TEACH YOURSELF

IDIOMS AND PHRASES

Edited by

ERIC WATSON

HIND POCKET BOOKS

An imprint of Penguin Random House

HIND POCKET BOOKS

USA | Canada | UK | Ireland | Australia
New Zealand | India | South Africa | China | Singapore

Hind Pocket Books is part of the Penguin Random House group of companies whose addresses can be found at global.penguinrandomhouse.com

Published by Penguin Random House India Pvt. Ltd
4th Floor, Capital Tower 1, MG Road,
Gurugram 122 002, Haryana, India

Penguin Random House India

First Published by Random House India in 2019
First published in Hind Pocket Books by Penguin Random House India 2023

10 9 8 7 6 5 4 3 2

ISBN 9789353492410

Printed at Repro India Limited

Preface

Idioms are those words or phrases in a language whose meaning cannot be taken literally. Thus, they defy grammatical or logical analysis. Yet, they are characteristic of a language and enrich it immensely. Since they are illogical, they have to be learnt and always pose problems to the second language learner.

There are great variations in the way that idioms can be used, and many of these variations are to be found in this book. The emphasis of this book is to create *an understanding of the meaning* of the idioms.

This book lists over 2,000 common and not so common English idioms, with their meanings clearly explained. To clarify the meaning further, each idiom has an example sentence, which also helps to show how the idiom can be used. Each is listed under a key word that forms part of the idiom, and cross-referenced under another significant word that it may contain. Thus, "haste makes waste" may be found both under 'haste' and 'waste'. The idioms are listed in alphabetical order.

It is always a problem to select the idioms, since in one sense all language is idiomatic, but the attempt for the most part has been to choose those idioms and phrases, *whose meanings cannot easiiy be worked out from the word they contain*. When it comes to understanding and learning English, it is these that are the greatest pitfalls, especially for the second language learner. It is hoped that all learners and users of English will find this book useful.

A

ABC. the ABC *beginning of something; elementary knowledge*

- George Bernard Shaw said at the age of ninety that he was still learning the ABC of politics.

ABACK. to be taken aback *to be surprised*

- He was taken aback when the tiger sprang out of the bush

ABANDON. to abandon oneself to *to be completely lost; ruined by a bad habit; to be given over to*

- We should see that young people do not abandon themselves to drugs.
- The prince had abandoned himself to his fate.

ABIDE. abide by *stick to*

- You must abide by your promise.

abide in *dwell*

- God abides in the hearts of righteous people.

ABODE. last abode *death (the grave)*

- His mother has gone to her last abode.

ABOUND. abound in *to have in plenty*

- The ocean abounds in fish of all kinds.
- A poor man's life abounds in trials and troubles of all kinds.

ABOUT. to be about *be busy at*

- What are you about?
- Get about your business.

ABOVE. over and above *besides, in addition to*

- I have parents to look after, over and above my children.

as above, so below *as in heaven, so on earth*

- Certain universal laws prevail as above, so below.

above all *besides everything else*

- He is rich, healthy and beautiful. Above all, he is lucky

above the earth *alive*

- A man has to do something as long as he is above the earth.

above board *honest and fair*

- The actions of successful politicians are seldom above board.
- All business transactions should be above board.

(Caesar's wife must be) above suspicion *big people should not merely be honest but should also seem to be honest, be known to be honest*

- Politicians, like Caesar's wife, should be above suspicion.

ABREAST. to keep abreast of *to be fully informed about; to be upto the mark*

- If you do not keep abreast of developments, you will lose out in your career.
- You must march/keep abreast of your competitors because in this world every man is for himself.

ACCESS. to have or gain access to *to have influence with*

- I have no access to the Prime Minister.
- You cannot get a good job unless you have some access to the appointing authority.

ACCOUNT. to account for *to be responsible for*

- If anything goes wrong, you will be called to account for it.

on account of *because of, for the sake of*

- Parents undergo great hardships on account of their children.

to be called to account *to die*

- Sooner or later, every one of us is called to account.

on account *to be paid for later*

- She bought a car on account.

ACE. **to be an ace in** *to be on top, to excel in*

- This lady is an ace in driving.
- He is an ace pilot.

ACID. **acid test** *the final proof*

- Public satisfaction is the acid test of a popular government.

ACME. **to be the acme of** *to be the highest point of*

- Contentment is the acme of progress.
- Truth is the acme of all knowledge.
- Her outfit is the acme of sophistication.

ACQUIT. **to acquit oneself well (or badly)** *to do well; to give a creditable performance*

- The Indian Army acquitted itself well in the war for the liberation of our neighbouring country.

ACROSS. **to come across** *to meet, to run into*

- I came across an old friend in the market.

ACT. **to act for** *to do the duty of, perform the work of*

- Who acts for you in your absence?

act of God *an unexpected event; accident; calamity*

- A flood is an act of God.

to act the ape *to behave like a fool*

- Don't act an ape when important discussions are going on.

to act upon *to work accordingly; to affect*

- You must act upon your mother's advice.
- Acid acts upon iron.

an act of grace *special favour*

- Good luck is an act of grace.
- Some people go unpunished just through an act of grace.

ACTION. **in action** *in operation*

- MISA is no longer in action.
- The law of *Karma* is always in action.

to take action against *to punish*

- The Government must take action against corrupt officers and businessmen.

out of action *no longer operative*

- Many repressive laws are now out of action.

ADAPT. to adapt oneself to *to get adjusted to*

- Immigrants must adapt themselves to new lifestyles.

ADD. to add to *increase*

- A death in the family adds to one's responsibilities.

ADDITION. in addition to *besides*

- I have no income in addition to what I earn from writing books.

ADEPT. to be adept at *to be perfect in; to be master of*

- Many an educated girl is quite adept at polished conversation.

ADHERE. to adhere to *to stick to; to perform; to implement*

- We must adhere to the spirit and not merely to the letter of the agreement.

ADIEU. to say adieu to *to bid goodbye to; to part from*

- You must now say adieu to lethargy and work hard to solve your domestic problems.

ADVANTAGE. to take advantage of *to make proper or full use of*

- You should take advantage of your high qualifications in getting a good job.

to be of advantage to *to be of help*

- Wealth is of no advantage to a dying person.

to take undue advantage of *to exploit*

- Many employers take undue advantage of poor illiterate labourers.

to have an advantage over *to be superior in some respect*

- Wealthy men have an advantage over men of high qualifications.

at an advantage *in a special or favourable situation*

- While competing for a job, the one with higher qualifications is at an advantage.

without advantage *without special favour*

- In politics, education is without advantage.

ADVOCATE. devil's advocate (to play the) *one who pursues an evil course for profit, an advocate at the papal court whose duty is to propose objections against a canonisation*

- Only the devil's advocate can declare corruption a legitimate part of business.

AEGIS. under the aegis of *under the patronage of*

- A big meeting was held at New Delhi under the aegis of the Socialist Forum.
- Crores of rupees were collected and misappropriated under the aegis of the new political party.

AFFAIR. to have an affair with *to be involved in a scandalous romance with*

- Lord Byron had an affair with Lady Caroline Lamb, as well as many society women.

none of one's affair *none of one's business*

- It is none of your affair whether I live or die.

AFFECTION. to have affection for *to love*

- Parents usually have great affection for their children.

AFFINITY. to have an affinity for *to be attracted to*

- Ram has a great affinity for Sheela.

- Hydrogen has great affinity for oxygen.
- Truth has no affinity for selfishness.

AGE. **under age** *not yet adult, below the minimum age*

- Persons who are under age cannot be employed in factories.

over age *above the prescribed age for employment, admission etc.*

- You cannot take a UPSC competitive examination even if you are over age by a single day.

from age to age *in all times*

- The victory of truth persists from age to age.

AGHAST. **to stand aghast** *to be surprised, astonished, shocked*

- When the thief snatched the gold chain, the lady stood aghast.

AGITATE. **to agitate against** *to launch a mass movement against*

- The people are agitating against rising prices and lawlessness.

AGREE. **to agree with** *to be of one mind with*

- I agree with you that the Iraqis committed aggression against Kuwait.

AGREEMENT. **to be in agreement with** *to agree*

- I am in agreement with your plan to join college for higher studies.

AIM. **to take aim at** *to make a target*

- The little boy took aim at the wild crow sitting on the hedge in his garden.

to have an aim in *to have personal interest or hope of gain in*

- What aim do you have in joining up with the criminals?

without aim *without purpose*

- Life without aim is meaningless.

AIR. **to take the air** *to refresh oneself in the open air*

- Old and retired people often come to take the air in municipal parks and public gardens.

to take to the air *to fly*

- The aeroplane soon took to the air.

AIRS. **to give oneself airs** *to be proud*

- Even if you have passed the examination creditably, do not give yourself airs.

ALL. **at all** *completely*

- I have no money at all.

in all *in the total, altogether*

- Twenty men were present in all.

all in all *absolute master of, altogether*

- The principal is all in all in the college.

above all *besides everything else*

- She is honest, good and true. Above all, she is beautiful.

all the same *nevertheless*

- Kumar passed his M.A. in the third division. All the same, he got a very good appointment in a multinational company.

all and sundry *everybody*

- The marriage reception was attended by all and sundry.

all at once *suddenly*

- All at once, there was a heavy downpour and the street was flooded.

ALOUD. **thinking aloud** *speaking out one's thoughts for one-self*

- Thinking aloud can sometimes be very risky.

ALTAR. **to bring to the altar or to lead up to the altar** *to marry*

- At last, he brought his beloved to the altar.

on the altar of *for the cause of*

- Millions have died on the altar of freedom.

AMBROSIA. **elixir and ambrosia** *divine food*

- Liquor and meat are elixir and ambrosia for a rich man.
- Money and power are elixir and ambrosia for a politician.

AMEN. **to say amen** *to approve*

- After listening to the leader's account of the strategy planned, all said 'Amen'.

AMOK. **to run amok** *to become mad*

- In the zest for pelf, power and possessions, many men have run amok.

ANCHOR. **at anchor** *standing still*

- The ship is at anchor in Bombay harbour.

to cast anchor *to berth a ship; to come to a stop*

- The social butterfly at last cast anchor when one of her favourites successfully persuaded her to marry him.

to weigh anchor *to start sailing off*

- After several years in college, the students finally weigh anchor and move into the ocean of adult life.

ANSWER. **to answer to** *to respond, to show signs of accepting as one's name*

- This dog answers to Timmy. (The name of the dog is Timmy.)

to answer the call of nature *to ease oneself, to go to the toilet*

- The villagers go out into the fields to answer the call of nature.

an answer to a prayer *fulfilment of a wish*

- Your coming is an answer to my prayers.

to answer one's purpose *to serve the purpose required*

- Your book answers my purpose.

- Most schools do not answer the purpose of true education.

in answer to *in response to*

- In answer to your advertisement, I beg to apply for a job in your esteemed office.

ANVIL. on the anvil *under discussion (being hammered into shape)*

- Many bills are on the anvil in Parliament at the moment.
- A new education policy is on the anvil.

ANY. any and every *all*

- Any and everyone can meet me here today.

APE. to play an ape to *to play the fool to*

- Do not play an ape to your employer.

to make an ape of *to befool*

- Do not make an ape of your friend.

ARAB. a street-Arab *a wandering boy*

- If you do not send your son to school, he will soon become a street Arab.

ARM/S. the arm of the law *the extent of authority*

- The arm of the law is very long.

arm in arm — *close together*

- Friends walk arm in arm on the Mall.

up in arms *fighting, in readiness to resist, protesting*

- Before independence, the whole nation was up in arms against the alien rulers of India.
- The students were up in arms at the expulsion of the class representative.

under arms *recruited in the army*

- In the war against Hitler, the British youth were under arms.

to lay down arms *to stop fighting, to surrender*

- On August 15, 1947, the British laid down their arms.

- The Germans laid down their arms to the Allied Army.\

to take to arms *to start fighting*

- At the slightest excuse, the Pathan tribes would take to arms in the North-West Frontier Province.

ARMED. to be armed to the teeth *to be fully armed*

- The dacoits were armed to the teeth when the police went to arrest them.

armed might *military strength*

- The armed might of the British Empire could not defeat the non-violent movement of Mahatma Gandhi.

ARROW. as the arrow (or crow) flies *in a straight line*

- Delhi is twelve miles from Ghaziabad as the arrow (or crow) flies.

to strike the arrow home *to achieve one's purpose*

- However strong you may be, you cannot strike the arrow home without good luck.

ATTENDANCE. to dance attendance on *to pamper and flatter*

- Many men dance attendance on ministers and powerful men.

AUSPICES. under the auspices of *under the patronage of*

- A mammoth meeting was held in Chandni Chowk under the auspices of the Progressive Party.

AUTUMN. in the autumn of life *in old age*

- The film star realized his dream of becoming the nation's matinee idol long before he reached the autumn of his life.

AWAKE. wide awake *fully vigilant*

- You have to be wide awake in the defence of freedom.

AWAY. to make away with *to rob and run away*

- The thief made away with my watch.

to do away with *kill, to dispose of*

- Stalin did away with his enemies.

AYE. **aye or nay** *yes or no*

- Whether you can help me or not, say aye or nay.

B

BABY. **to hold the baby** *to bear responsibility*

- Nobody wants to hold the baby when an important decision is to be taken on a vital national matter.
- When the minister is away, his deputy has to hold the baby.

BACHELOR. **to play the bachelor** *to pretend to be unmarried.*

- Many widowers play the bachelor in the matrimonial columns.

BACK. **back down** *to abandon one's opinion or position*

- When the minister was confronted with the facts, he backed down about the riots.

back up *support*

- India backed up Bangladesh against Pakistan.

at the back of *behind*

- The bodyguard was at the back of the minister.

back number *an out-of-date method or person*

- In this age of tractors, a plough is a back number.
- With swiftly changing fashions, it is difficult not to become a back number.

back out *to withdraw, to evade an obligation or undertaking*

- India cannot back out of her international obligations.

take a back seat *to efface or humble oneself*

- The vain and glorious leader is always unwilling to take a back seat.

BACKBONE. to be the backbone of *to be the main support, helper, mainstay, etc.*

- Truth is the backbone of true philosophy.
- My elder son is the backbone of the family.

BACKDOOR. backdoor policy *secret controlling power, unworthily clandestine*

- A backdoor policy does not pay in politics.

to make a backdoor entry *to enter a position by unfair methods*

- Many influential people make a backdoor entry into lucrative posts.

BACKHANDED. backhanded blow *stroke delivered with the back of the hand, sarcastic, indirect, insincere*

- Politicians usually destroy their enemies with backhanded blows.

BACKWATERS. in the backwaters of *behind, in an inferior position*

- Journalists glorify themselves in the backwaters of politics.

BAD. to go bad *to become rotten, to decompose*

- The egg has gone bad.
- Food goes bad quickly in the heat.

go to the bad *go to moral ruin*

- Her affairs with men ultimately made her go to the bad.

from bad to worse *gradual deterioration*

- Education is going from bad to worse today.
- The power situation is going from bad to worse, leading to frequent loadshedding.

big bad wolf *the fear of the unknown*

- She was not afraid of the big bad wolf.

BADGE. badge of honour *mark of distinction*

- For a patriot, imprisonment is a badge of honour.

BAFFLE. to baffle the best brains *to outwit everybody*

- The criminals sometimes baffle the best brains in the police.
- The puzzles in the Sunday columns often baffle the best brains.

BAG. to have in the bag *to almost get a thing*

- After winning the primary elections, Kennedy had the Presidency in the bag.

to buy a cat in the bag *to be cheated*

- Influenced by a shopkeeper's sales pitch, quite often we buy a cat in the bag.

to let the cat out of the bag *the secret is out*

- Finally the cat is out of the bag and everybody knows what happened during the war.
- The cat is out of the bag with regard to the sugar scandal.

bag and baggage *completely, with all belongings*

- The British left India bag and baggage on August 15, 1947.

BAIL. to stand bail for *to give a surety in court*

- When your friend is in police custody, you have to stand bail for him.

on bail *released because of someone's surety.*

- His friend is on bail these days.

to bail out *helped out of difficulties*

- The prisoner was bailed out by his accomplices.

BAIT. to serve as a bait *offer allurement or temptation to trap somebody*

- Wealth, wine and women serve as baits even for the most righteous people sometimes.

BALANCE. to lose one's balance *to become unstable*

- Anger very often makes one lose one's balance.

to throw one off one's balance *to make one discontented and unhappy*

- The death of his son threw him off his balance.

BALANCE-SHEET. the balance-sheet of life *success and failure*

- You find many pluses and minuses in the balance-sheet of life.
- Many things add up to make the balance-sheet of life.

BALL. to set the ball rolling *to get things going*

- Somebody should set the ball rolling before a marriage can be arranged.
- Once I have set the ball rolling, you must carry on with this work.

the ball to be in someone's court *someone's responsibility for the next move*

- For further discussions between us, the ball is in your court.

BALLED. balled up *(of speaker) confused and so unable to go on*

- When the police interrogated the suspect, he was quite balled up.

BANDY. to bandy words *to argue*

- It does not pay to bandy words with your employer.
- Many teenagers enjoy bandying words with those in authority.

BANK. to bank upon *depend upon*

- One has to bank upon somebody in times of adversity.

BANKRUPT. to go bankrupt *lose all assets due to court action*

- Speculators quite often go bankrupt.

BARGAIN. to strike a bargain *to make a bargain*

- He struck a bargain and bought a dog for one hundred rupees.

in the bargain *along with other things*

- He married, and got a stepson in the bargain.

BASKET. pick of the basket *the best thing available*

- When fruit was distributed, he always got the pick of the basket.

BAT. to bat an eyelid *to express displeasure or surprise*

- When the police took away his son, he did not bat an eyelid.

bat round *to have a good time*

- When the teacher was away, the boys were batting round.

BATHE. bathe in *(figurative use) completely covered or drenched*

- The valley was bathed in sunshine.
- Her cheek was bathed in tears.
- "Every morning, I bathed my intellect in the *Bhagavad Gita,"* said Henry David Thoreau, the great American philosopher.

BATHOS. pathos and bathos *emotional ups and downs*

- Life is full of pathos and bathos.

BATTLES. battles lost and won *the ups and downs of life*

- He became a leader after many battles lost and won.

BAY. to stand at bay *to face the enemy boldly*

- When the dog attacked the kitten, the cat stood at bay.

to bring to bay *to corner for a fight*

- The hounds brought the fox to bay after a long chase.
- The police brought the smuggler to bay on a deserted street.

at bay *said of hunted animals surrounded by dogs and unable to escape; also applied to human beings in a similar situation*

- When her lover's relations harassed her, the girl found herself at bay.

BE. to be or not to be *to live or to die*

- "To be or not to be — that is the question," said Hamlet in the Shakespearean play, *Hamlet.* (not in current use)

BEADS. to pray over the beads *to use a rosary for prayers*

- Old folk pray over the beads.

BEAM. to see the mote in another's eye but not the beam in one's own (a Biblical allusion) *to criticise others for small faults but ignore one's own big faults*

- Politicians see the mote in another's eye but not the beam in their own.

BEAR. bear garden *a scene of tumult or turmoil*

- The communalists turned the temple into a bear garden.
- The college was turned into a bear garden after the riots.

to bear fruit *to yield happy results*

- Good efforts always bear fruit.

to bear the brunt of the battle *to endure the greater part of a stress or burden.*

- In the struggle for independence, Uttar Pradesh bore the brunt of the battle.

BEAST. beast of burden *one who bears a heavy responsibility*

- The mother in the family is often a beast of burden.

BEAT. to beat about the bush *to evade the issue, to approach a subject indirectly*

- If you want to win your point, it is no use beating about the bush.
- When the student couldn't think of a suitable excuse, he started beating about the bush.

BEATEN. to follow the beaten path *to do as others have done, to follow tradition*

- In religion, millions follow the beaten path.

- People prefer to follow the beaten path when marrying their children in India.

BEAU. beau geste *a display of magnanimity, gracious gesture*

- Marriage often demands a beau geste.
- When the school announced a special scholarship for the motherless girl, everyone appreciated the beau geste.

BEAUTY. beauty sleep *sleep before midnight, considered the most refreshing*

- Few people in the West ever think of their beauty sleep.
- After several late nights, most ladies like to catch up on their beauty sleep.

BED. a bed of roses *easy or comfortable place, a cushioned existence*

- Life is not a bed of roses.

a bed of thorns *hard existence*

- The *yogis* prefer a bed of thorns.
- Her husband was an invalid and her life was really a bed of thorns.

BEDPOST. between you, me and the bedpost *limited to myself and you alone*

- Between you, me and the bedpost, no one will know this secret.

BEDROCK. bedrock *foundation, fundamental principles*

- Civilization stands on the bedrock of industry.

BEE-LINE. bee-line *straight line between two places, the most direct road*

- The picnickers made a bee-line for the playground.
- Most school children make a bee-line for home after school (They go straight home.)

BEG. to beg the question *to assume by implication the very fac one is trying to prove*

- To define man as a human being is to beg the question.

BEGGAR. **beggar description** *to be beyond description*

- The outfits displayed at the fashion show beggared description.

beggar-my-neighbour *a card game, that goes on until one has gained all the others' cards; an endless rigmarole*

- Life is nothing but a sort of beggar-my-neighbour.

BEHIND. **to be behind hand** *in arrears, tardy*

- You are behind hand in your payments.

behind time *late*

- I am behind time for school today.
- The monsoon is often behind time in North India.

behind one's back *in one's absence*

- One should not criticise anybody behind his back.

BELIEVE. **believe it or not** *very strange but true, extraordinary*

- Believe it or not, there were once flying snakes in India.

BELOW. **to hit below the belt** *hit in an unfair manner, to attack unfairly*

- You should not hit even your enemy below the belt.

below one's dignity *dishonourable,* infra dig *(Latin)*

- It is not below one's dignity to walk one's way home or to earn one's living.

BENCH. **the bench and the bar** *the body or assembly of barristers or advocates collectively*

- Law is what the bench and the bar make it.
- The role of the bench and bar in maintaining public morality is often not very great.

BEND. **to bend, not break** *to meet dishonour rather than death, to yield, not to be inflexible*

- It is better to bend than to break.

BETIDE. betide me well, betide me woe *whether I am happy or sad*

- Betide me well, betide me woe, I will not let you down.

BIG. big bug *important person*

- He is a big bug nowadays.

to talk big *to boast*

- Those who talk big soon lose all credibility.
- People with newly acquired wealth often talk big.

BIGWIG. bigwig *important person, a leading man*

- The bigwigs fill our Parliament.

BIND. to bind hand and foot *to tie up effectively or with assiduous attention*

- They bound the notorious criminal hand and foot while taking him to jail.

fast bind, fast find *the more secure a thing is, the more easily it can be found when necessary*

- Fast bind money, fast find money.

BIRDS. birds of passage *migratory birds, tourists*

- Delhi is full of birds of passage.

bird's-eye view *as seen from above*

- From the window of our hotel, we had a bird's-eye view of Bombay.
- The high-rise buildings give a bird's-eye view of the city.

BIT. bit by bit *little by little*

- You can do difficult work bit by bit.

BLIND. blind alley *a path that leads nowhere, cul de sac*

- The unemployed often find themselves in a blind alley.

to turn a blind eye *to ignore*

- The fond mother turned a blind eye to the misdoings of her only son.

blind man's buff *a game in which a blindfolded man tries to catch others*

- Life is a sort of blind man's buff.

BLOOD. **blood for blood** *punishment equal to crime, tit for tat*

- Modern justice does not advocate the principle of blood for blood.

blood cries out *murder cannot be hidden*

- The murderer is caught sooner or later, for blood cries out.

to shed blood *to murder, to kill*

- Timur shed much blood in India.
- Despite Gandhi's efforts, people did not hesitate to shed blood during the Partition.

blood is thicker than water *kith and kin are dearer than friends or acquaintances*

- The minister exonerated his son since blood is thicker than water.
- The teacher favoured his nephew, for blood is thicker than water, after all.

BLOW. **to blow in** *to turn up casually*

- People blew in at the poetry recital.

BLUE. **to beat black and blue** *to punish severely*

- The irate teacher beat the boy black and blue.

true blue—*aristocratic, faithful to blue-blooded principles*

- Members of the I.C.S. considered themselves true blue.
- The corporate bosses are now emerging as the true blues in modern society.

BOW. **to have many strings to one's bow** *to achieve one's purpose in different ways*

- A politician has many strings to his bow.

BOX. **to box the compass** *(i.e. to name the 32 points of the* *compass in their order and then backwards), to make a complete roundabout in one's opinion, etc.*

- The so-called intelligentsia in coffee houses often box the compass.
- When necessary, politicians will even box the compass rather than lose their seats

BRAIN. brain or brawn *intellectual or physical strength*

- Brain or brawn, you must get on with the job.
- Modern farming methods make both brain and brawn necessary for success.

BREAST. breast to breast *side by side*

- The soldiers marched breast to breast.
- After the recent earthquake the army and civilian volunteers marched breast to breast in rehabilitation work.

to make a clean breast of *to reveal everything, to confess without reservations*

- The culprit made a clean breast of everything in the court to save his skin.
- Their daughter made a clean breast of her love affair.

BRIM. full to the brim *full completely*

- His cup of misery was full to the brim;
- Her heart was full to the brim with joy.

BRING. to bring about *to cause*

- The Ayurvedic medicine brought about a great change in her condition.
- Bringing about a change in attitudes is necessary for ushering in social changes.

to bring off *to succeed in*

- Sunil Gavaskar brought off a great victory for India in the Test Match.

- The diplomats brought off a great success in Geneva recently.

BUCKET. to kick the bucket *to die*

- Sooner or later, everyone must kick the bucket.

BULL. to take the bull by the horns *to take bold action, to overcome a difficulty*

- If trouble befalls you, it is best to take the bull by the horns.
- The alcoholic's wife decided to take the bull by the horns and took him to a psychiatric clinic for de-addiction.

a red rag to the bull *cause of annoyance or provocation*

- A fat man in a hungry crowd is a red rag to the bull.

to be a bull in a China shop *to destroy wantonly, to lack the delicacy that the situation calls for*

- Chengiz Khan in Delhi was a veritable bull in a China shop.

BURN. to burn the candle at both ends *to waste or use up in two ways at once; to waste both health and wealth; to work too hard*

- When youth burn the candle at both ends, they pay for it dearly in old age.
- Students usually resort to burning the candle at both ends as the examinations draw near.

BUT. but me no buts *don't argue with me, raise no objections. (no longer in colloquial use.)*

- When I tell you to be off, but me no buts.

BY. by and by *gradually*

- By and by, the children grew up.

BYGONES. to let bygones be bygones *to forget former differences*

- Let bygones be bygones and let us begin life anew.
- The rivals decided to let bygones be by gones and patched up their quarrel.

C

CAD. a cad *a low, ill-bred dishonourable person, a low vulgar chap.*

- Education hides many a cad.

CAKE. to eat one's cake and have it *to want to have the advantage of both the alternatives*

- You cannot eat the cake and have it too.

CALL. call up *summon from beneath or from another world to a tribunal, to the colours, to memory*

- All the soldiers were called up for active service on the outbreak of hostilities.

call up *(modern colloquial) to telephone*

- I'll call you up sometime tomorrow.

call down *to invoke; to rebuke*

- The Prophet called down curses on the sinners.
- The officer called down the workers for negligence.

call to account *summon to render an account, hold responsible for*

- The behaviour of the rebels during the war is being called to account.

CAN. from can-see to can't see *from dawn to dusk*

- The labourers work from can-see to can't see.

CAP. to cap it all *to sum up, to top it all*

- To cap it all, corruption was rampant in the king's regime.

CAPE. Cape boy *Negro, a South African half-breed*

- Cape boys have been denied democratic liberties in South Africa for long.

CAPERS. to cut capers *to run, to execute a frisk*

- The youngsters cut capers in school.

CAPITAL. to make capital out of *to take advantage of*

- It is against medical ethics to make capital out of people's sufferings.

with a capital letter *emphatically*

- Bombay is a big city with a capital letter.
- His creations are high-fashion in capital letters.

capital mistake *big blunder*

- It was a capital mistake for America to think that it could defeat Cuba.

CAPTAIN. captain of (one's) destiny *master of one's fate*

- No mortal is captain of his destiny forever.

CAREER. to carve out one's career *to find one's proper work in life*

- It is everyone's duty to carve out his career in life.

CARPET. on the carpet *under discussion*

- The abolition of *zamindari* was on the carpet in the House at that moment.

CARROT. to hold a carrot on a stick *to promise a reward after performance of duty*

- The leader's statement was a carrot held out on a stick for the union workers.

CARRY. carry all before oneself *to bear down all obstacles*

- Sujata carried all before her and married the boy of her choice.

carry over — *the balance of account which is taken over to the next day*

- Rupees ten were carried over.

carry forward *march forward; progress*

- Every generation carries the nation forward.

to carry through *to win, to succeed through difficulties*

- Great men carry through despite all obstacles.

to carry home *to impress, to emphasise*

- It was carried home to the leaders that food was as important to the masses as freedom.

CART. **to put the cart before the horse** *to do things in a wrong way, or in the wrong order of priority*

- The difference between democracy and dictatorship is that the former puts the horse before the cart and the latter puts the cart before the horse.

CARTE-BLANCHE. **carte-blanche** *(a blank paper, duly signed, to be filled up at the recipient's pleasure), freedom of action*

- The general gave a carte-blanche to his soldiers when they crossed the frontier into enemy territory.

CARTOON. **to make a cartoon of** *to make one a subject of laughter*

- The managing director resented being made a cartoon of.
- The child made a cartoon of himself when his mother had visitors.

CASH. **to cash in (1)** *to settle accounts, to exchange counters for money on leaving the gambling-table*

- You can cash in during office hours.

to cash in (2) *to die (more in use than (1) now)*

- After a prolonged illness, he finally cashed in.

cash on *to take advantage of*

- The fallen leader is trying to cash on his former glory and
- success.

cash down *payment across the table*

- You can earn a big discount when you pay cash down.

CAST. **cast away** *get rid of*

- We should cast away untouchability and other odious customs.

cast down *frustrated*

- Arjuna was cast down before Lord Krishna delivered the sermon of the *Bhagavad Gita* to him to raise his spirits.

cast in one's lot with *to share the destiny of*

- The leaders must not stand apart from the mainstream but cast in their lot with the teeming millions.

cast into the shade *to overshadow, to eclipse*

- Birbal cast Akbar into the shade.

cast an eye on *to eye, to look at greedily*

- The ruffians cast an eye on the widow's wealth.

cast anchor *to halt a ship, to make a stop*

- The ship cast anchor at Bombay.

casting-vote *a deciding vote in case of equality of other votes*

- The chairman of a committee enjoys the casting-vote.

CASTE. without caste, colour and creed *without any distinction*

- We should believe in universal brotherhood without any considerations of caste, colour and creed.

CASTLES. build castles in the air or in Spain *to make wild plans, or groundless or visionary projects*

- The child was building castles in the air when he imagined himself to be a superman.

CASUALTY. become a casualty *to die because of*

- Truth is the first casualty in war.

CAT. cat's-paw *a person used as a tool by another*

- The petty thief became a cat's-paw in the hands of his gang leader.

lead a cat-and-dog life *to be always bickering and quarrelling*

- Many a married couple lead a cat-and-dog life.

CATCH. catchpenny *worthless things intended merely to sell, claptrap*

- Many manufactured products in the market are merely catchpennies.

catchword *watchword or symbol of a group or party, catchy phrase in politics, etc.*

- Socialism and *Ramarajya* are great catchwords.

CATER. cater to *provide food, entertainment, etc.*

- Five-star hotels mainly cater to foreign tourists, or to those with expense accounts.

CABBAGE. as cabbage to cauliflower *an inferior product to a superior one*

- An educated person is to an illiterate man as a cabbage to cauliflower.
- "A cabbage is a cauliflower without college education," said Mark Twain.

cabbages and kings *a wide range of topics, from people and the aristocracy (quotation from Lewis Carroll)*

- Certain people can talk of literally everything from cabbages to kings.

CHAIN. chain of events *a series of occurrences happening one after the other*

- The German Government stage-managed a chain of events before proclaiming war.

CHALK. not to know chalk from cheese *to know nothing about the matter*

- The two brothers were as different as chalk from cheese.
- Illusion differs from reality as chalk from cheese but many eat chalk without ever having eaten cheese.

CHALLENGE. to meet the challenge *to face danger*

- In case of war, we rally round to meet the challenge.

CHAMELEON. a political chameleon *one who changes views and parties*

- A defector is a political chameleon.

CHANGE. a quick-change artist *one who changes views, dress, appearance, etc. quickly*

- A fashion-lover has to be a quick-change artist.

CHAOS. from cosmos to chaos *from order to disorder*

- Lawlessness leads from cosmos to chaos.
- God rules supreme from cosmos to chaos.

CHAPTER. to open a new chapter *to make a fresh beginning*

- With independence, India opened a new chapter in her history.

CHARACTER. character assassination *bringing someone a bad name by exposing deficiencies of character, defaming someone*

- Politicians often indulge in the character assassination of their antagonists.
- Character assassination is common practice in politics.

CHARIOT. chariot wheel *great grinding power*

- Everyone is ground under the chariot wheel of a tyrannous government.

CHARTER. charter barter *exchanging written grants of rights and privileges*

- Marriage is no charter barter, it is a sacrament.

CHECK. check in *to register one's entry*

- They checked in at the hotel.

check out *leave a hotel, have a look at*

- The teenager said to his friends, "Lets go and check out the new disco."

- Guests usually have to check out of their hotel rooms by 12 noon.

CHEW. chew Jew *one who robs you slowly*

- A shopkeeper is a chew Jew.

CHICKEN. chicken feed *small quantity of food, small amount of money*

- A quintal is chicken feed for an elephant.
- The salaries we drew in our youth seem mere chicken feed to our children.

CHIFF-CHAFF. chiff-chaff *small warbler*

- A wandering *sadhu* is a chiff-chaff.

CHIME. to chime in *to say ditto, to join in, in agreement*

- When the minister says something, the secretary chimes in.

CHIP. chip of the old block *one with the characteristics of his father*

- A child is usually a chip of the old block.
- Mr. M. F. Husain's son seems to be a chip of the old block.

CHISEL. chisel one's way/career *make progress slowly*

- Don't expect to become President overnight. You will have to chisel out your career in politics.

CHITCHAT. chitchat *light talk, gossip*

- Social chitchat should accompany a good dinner.
- While at work, one should not engage in chitchat.

CLAM. to clam up *to become uncommunicative, to stop talking*

- When the journalists started asking leading questions, the film-star clammed up.

COCK. a cock-and-bull story *a cooked up story, a fabrication*

- Dennis cooked up a cock-and-bull story to explain his rosence from school.

COME. **come devil, come God** *Whatever may happen*

- He decided to rise to the top, come devil, come God.

to come to terms *to agree on some basis, to compromise*

- The socialists and the democrats at last came to terms.

to stage a comeback *to return to a former position*

- Many discredited politicians are trying to stage a comeback

to come to grips with *to tackle*

- The new Prime Minister has not yet come to grips with the problems of his people.

to come up *to show progress*

- The boy will come up by and by.

to come down heavily upon *punish*

- The officers came down heavily upon the staff for the accident.

a come-down *defeat, humiliation*

- It was a great come-down for him.

COMMIT. **to commit oneself to** *to agree to do something*

- We have committed ourselves to helping you in your distress.

COMMON. **to make common cause with** *to cast in one's lot with, to have the same interest and aims with*

- The Communist Party made common cause with the Socialists to form a government.

COMPLIMENT. **to pay a compliment to** *to praise, to appreciate*

- They paid many compliments to the leader when he returned from a successful foreign tour.

to pay a left-handed compliment *to say a thing intended to seem a compliment but in reality the reverse*

- The principal paid a left-handed compliment to the new teacher.

- Many left-handed compliments are exchanged at kitty parties.

COMPROMISE. to compromise one's honour *to do something dishonourable*

- Unlike most people today, the workman never compromised his honour.

CONCLUSION. to draw a conclusion or to come to the conclusion *to draw an inference or form judgement*

- There are no moral lessons in a modern story but you can draw your own conclusions.

CONCOCTED. concocted tale *a cooked up story, a fabrication*

- The revolutionary leader asserted that his so-called plan to murder leaders of the government was a concocted tale.

CONFESSION. to make a confession *reveal the truth*

- The convict has made a confession in court.

CONSPIRE. to conspire with *to join hands in an anti-social enterprise*

- The rebels conspired with the police to kill the prime minister.

CONTEMPT. to hold in contempt *to hate, to hold in scorn*

- Dishonourable people are held in contempt by everyone.

CONTRARY. contrary to *against*

- What you said now is contrary to your statement yesterday.

COPE. to cope with *tackle, to manage (Most people tend to use the intrusive preposition "up". This is incorrect.)*

- A modern man cannot cope with his day-to-day problems.

CORE. to the core of one's heart *completely*

- The village *patwari* is sincere to the core of his heart.

COST. at a heavy cost *with much loss*

- India liberated Bangladesh at a heavy cost.

at no cost — *with no effort, free*

- He won success in life at no cost.

cost what it may *whatever may be the price*

- Napoleon and Hitler decided to conquer Russia, cost what it may.

COSTLY. costly enterprise *an expensive venture*

- Attaining success in life is a costly enterprise.

COW. to cow down *to frighten*

- You cannot cow down a righteous man.
- The bully tried to cow down his weak victim.

CRACKAJACK. crackajack or crackerjack *a person of highest excellence*

- Dr. Homi Bhabha was a crackajack.

CRADLE. from the cradle to the grave *throughout one's life*

- Man is born to suffer from the cradle to the grave.

CRAM. to cram up *to learn by rote*

- The students cram up their books without understanding a word in order to do well in the examination.

CRASH. crash programme *a plan to be executed quickly.*

- Soviet Russia devised many crash programmes to step up economic development.

CREST. on the crest of *on the top of*

- Julius Caesar rode to power on the crest of a victory in battle.

CRISS. criss-cross *intertwines; crossing and recrossing entangled*

- The course of life runs in a criss-cross manner.

CROCODILE. crocodile tears *false suffering, hypocritical grief*

- Many beggars shed crocodile tears to seek alms.

- When he died, a lot of sycophants shed crocodile tears.

CUT. **cut no ice** *to affect little or nothing*

- Whatever the criminal stated cut no ice in court.
- The student's lame excuses cut no ice with the principal.

D

DANDY. **a Jack-a-dandy** *fop; a very fashionable person*

- Public schools are full of many a Jack-a-dandy.

DEAF. **deaf to** *indifferent to*

- The bureaucracy is deaf to the pleas and sufferings of the poor.

DEBT. **debt of honour** *loan without legal document*

- Even thieves pay their debts of honour.

debt of gratitude *profound thankfulness*

- You have laid us under a heavy debt of gratitude.

DEEP. **to be in deep waters** *to be in trouble*

- The king was in deep waters because of his wayward temperament.
- The Government is in deep waters because of its own short-sighted policies.

DEFECT. **defect of quality** *a shortcoming due to greatness*

- Absentmindedness is a defect of quality.

DEFERENCE. **in deference to** *because of respect for*

- He went on a pilgrimage in deference to the wishes of his mother.

DEFLATE. **to deflate one's ego** *to cut one down to size*

- The conqueror's ego was deflated by his final defeat.

DEGREE. **to a degree** *to some extent*

- Everybody is a slave to a degree.

DELIVER. to deliver the goods *to fulfil pledges*

- The manager is trying to deliver the goods.
- You have to be able to deliver the goods if you want to succeed in business.

DELIVERED. to be delivered of *to be rid of*

- I will be glad to be delivered of this headache.

DELUGE. after me, the deluge (the original is in French "Apres moi, c'est deluge") *I do not mind if the whole world suffers so long as I am quite safe*

- The King said, "After me, the deluge."

DELUSIONS. illusions and delusions *false hopes*

- We all suffer from many illusions and delusions.

DELUXE. deluxe *of unusual sumptuousness*

- They gave us a dinner *deluxe.*
- They reserved a deluxe apartment for him.

DELVE. delve deep *search hard*

- We have to delve deep for the truth.

DEMI. to become a demi-god *to be more than human and less than godly.*

- Many leaders have become demi-gods, even in their own eyes.

DESTINY. man of destiny *man who decides the future*

- Garibaldi was Italy's man of destiny.

DEUS. deus ex machina *divine interposition or other artificial solution of difficulties*

- Fidel Castro has proved to be *deus ex machina* for Cuba's political difficulties.

DEVIL. devil-may-care *happy-go-lucky; irrepressible*

- She had a devil-may-care attitude to life.

DEVOUR. **to devour a book** *to read a book quickly*

- My wife devours a novel a day.

DIAMOND. **diamond of the first water** *very precious, with many intrinsic good qualities*

- My friend is a diamond of the first water.

DILLY. **dilly-dally** *procrastinate or vacillate*

- If you want to achieve success, stop dilly-dallying.

DIM. **to have a dim view of things** *to be pessimistic, to be disapproving*

- It does not pay to have a dim view of things.
- Most parents take a dim view of their children's late nights.

DINE. **to wine and dine** *to enjoy eats and drinks*

- They dined and wined at the Royal party.

DUTY. **discharge one's duty** *to do one's allotted work*

- You should discharge your duty diligently.

DISH. **to dish out a story** *to give interesting news*

- Every newspaper dishes out stories of current interest.

DISTRESS. **damsel in distress** *a lady in trouble*

- He rushed to the rescue of the damsel in distress.

DO. **do-nothing** *idle*

- Do-nothing boys loiter around the streets these days.

do's and don'ts *things to be done and avoided*

- Every school has its do's and don'ts.
- Most ladies pick up the do's and don'ts of fashion very fast.

to do or die *to work desperately for success*

- In these days of high unemployment, one must do or die.

do up *decorate*

- The Christmas tree was beautifully done up by the children.
- I'm planning to do up the living room soon.

do as you would be done by *treat others as you wish to be treated*

- If you want to be happy, do as you would be done by.

DOG. dog-tired *completely tired; very much fatigued*

- I was really dog-tired when I went to bed last night.

DOLDRUMS. in the doldrums *in trouble*

- He is still in the doldrums.

DOVETAIL. to dovetail into *to join together by intermixing, to fit in*

- The past is dovetailed into the future.
- Their programmes dovetailed beautifully.

DOWN. ups and downs *vicissitudes of life*

- Life is full of ups and downs.

to be down at the heels *to be poverty-stricken*

- Millions of our people are leading a down-at-the-heel existence.

to be run down *to wear out, lose one's health, drained of vitality*

- You seem to be run down nowadays.

Down Under *at the antipodes, Australia*

- She has gone Down Under.

down and down *gradually decaying*

- Business is going down and down.

Down with *put down*

- Down with terrorists!
- 'Down with male chauvinism' is the war-cry of the feminist movement.

to down one's tools *to stop work*

- The workers downed their tools and went home.

to let down *desert*

- Don't let down your friends in trouble.

to be cast down *to feel frustrated, dejected or depressed in mind*

- You seem cast down today.

down-and-out *at the end of one's resources, completely beaten or frustrated*

- Many educated men often become down-and-out owing to unemployment.

DRACONIAN. Draconian laws *severe regulations*

- Draconian laws were enforced during war-time all over British India.

DRAG. to drag one's feet *to make a slow retreat*

- The Chinese Army was dragging its feet in Vietnam.

DRAIN. brain-drain *loss of educated and intelligent workers through emigration*

- India suffers heavily from brain-drain every year, as people seek better employment abroad.

DRAW. to draw together *to be attracted*

- Dissimilar people rarely draw together, despite the attraction of opposites.

to end in a draw *with no party (or neither of two) winning*

- The cricket match ended in a draw.

DRESS. to dress down *to handle with severity; to reprimand; to take to task*

- You can get no work done without dressing down the illiterate workers.

DRINK. to drink to someone's health *to drink wine as a toast*

- They drank to the health of the business tycoon.

to drink deep *to study carefully*

- Drink deep at the fountain of knowledge.

DROWNED. to be drowned in tears *to be overwhelmed with sorrow*

- After the death of her husband, the woman was drowned in tears.

DUEL. cruel duel *a hard hand-to-hand fight*

- One has to fight a cruel duel with destiny before one comes out with flying colours.

DUMPTY. humpty-dumpty *a short, squat, egg-like being of nursery folklore; a gypsy drink, ale boiled with brandy; a vast unmanageable enterprise; a great empire*

- That woman is a humpty-dumpty.
- Lenin vanquished the humpty-dumpty Tsarist empire.

DUPE. dope and dupe *drug and cheat*

- The youth are doped and duped by the false promises of politicians.

DUSK. from dawn to dusk *from morning to evening*

- A labourer works for his living from dawn to dusk.

DYED. dyed in *fully tinged with and confirmed*

- A Communist is dyed in the ideology of his party.

DYNAMO. dynamo of power *person of great energy*

- A prime minister needs to be a dynamo of power.

E

EAGLE. eagle's-eye view *picture from high up in the sky*

- We had an eagle's-eye view of the city from the top of the skyscraper.

EARNEST. in right earnest *serious, very keen, eager*

- He is in right earnest about the staging of his play.

EARTH. born of earth *mortal*

- All things born of earth must perish.

down to earth *practical; not imaginary*

- Our thinking must be down to earth.
- We should lead down-to-earth lives.

from the earth to the sky *everywhere*

- Truth prevails from the earth to the sky.

below the earth *dead and gone*

- Many of our friends are now below the earth.

earth, earthly *mortal*

- All things of earth, (earthly,) must perish.

EASE. to be at ease *to feel comfortable*

- Please be at ease here in our house.

EAT. to eat humble pie *to be humiliated*

- The Prime Minister had to eat humble pie when he couldn't fulfil his promises.

to eat one's words *to retract, to deny what one has said*

- Politicians often have to eat their words.

EBB. ebb and flow *ups and downs*

- There is an ebb and flow in the tide of every man's life.

ECHO. to echo in the corridors of time *to be heard in history*

- The words of Mahatma Gandhi will echo in the corridors of time.

EDDIES. eddies and whirlpools *troubles and storms*

- We all have to swim through the eddies and whirlpools of this transitory pilgrimage of life.

EDEN. Garden of Eden *paradise*

- Technology has yet to produce a Garden of Eden on earth.

EDGE. to have an edge over *to have an advantage over*

- The children of rich families have an edge over poor students in many ways.

EDITION. deluxe edition *sumptuous, well-bound, well-produced, costly edition (usually of a book)*

- This is a deluxe edition of the *Bhagavad Gita.*

EGG. a bad egg *worthless person*

- Despite his good schooling, the boy turned out to be a bad egg.

to put all one's eggs in one basket *to risk all on one enterprise*

- A wise man never puts all his eggs in one basket.

to egg on *to incite, to urge*

- Lady Macbeth egged on her husband to murder the king.

EKE. to eke out one's living *to make one's livelihood with difficulty*

- With all my labour, I barely manage to eke out my living.

ELAN. elan vital *idealism plus a lust for living*

- Jawaharlal Nehru advocated the development of elan vital among the youth of the country.

ELBOW. out at the elbow *coat ragged at the elbows; poor, worn out, torn clothes*

- Millions in Indian wear clothes which are out at the elbow.

EL DORADO. El Dorado *The golden land of imagination of the Spanish conquerors of America; any place where wealth is to be easily made*

- Bombay is an El Dorado for aspiring film stars.

ELEMENT. in one's element *in high spirits*

- Nehru was always in his element while at work.
- Michael Jackson is a born performer and is in his element while on stage.

ELEPHANT. **a white elephant** *anything that gives more trouble than it is worth; too costly to maintain*

- The gift of a car to a poor man becomes a white elephant for him.

ELEVENTH. **at the eleventh hour** *at the last moment*

- My brother reached the hospital at the eleventh hour, just when my mother was being moved to the operation theatre.

ENCROACH. **encroach upon** *to intrude upon others' territory*

- The rich must not encroach upon the rights and privileges of the poor.

END. **to be at one's wit's end** *to be confused or perplexed; not to know what to do in a certain situation*

- I was at my wit's end when my mother died suddenly.
- I'm at my wit's end trying to figure out this problem.

to make two ends meet *to live within one's income*

- It is hard for a poor man to make two ends meet.
- Most families now need two incomes to make two ends meet.

the end of the world *death (figuratively)*

- It was the end of the world for him.
- Losing a job is not the end of the world.

means and ends *resources and results*

- Means and ends count a great deal in life. Good ends must be achieved by good means.
- "Does the end always justify the means?" is a question that frequently confronts us.

to this end *to this purpose*

- He worked hard to this end that his family should not starve.

ENGINES. **engines of war** *military hardware*

- No nation can today avoid equipping itself with the engines of war.

ENIGMA. an enigma in a riddle *very complicated question*

- Death is an enigma in a riddle.

ENOUGH. enough and to spare *plenty*

- There is food enough and to spare in our kitchen.

EN ROUTE. en route *on the way*

- I met my friend en route to school.

ENTER. enter into an agreement *to sign a pact*

- India has entered into an agreement with many countries.

ENTIRE. to one's entire satisfaction *completely satisfactory*

- You will find my work to your entire satisfaction.

to be entirely at someone's disposal *to be fully at the service of*

- I am entirely at your disposal from today.

ENTRANCE. to gain an entrance *to enter*

- It is no small matter to gain entrance into a college in Delhi.

EQUAL. equal to the task *competent to do a particular work*

- The young professor proved himself equal to the task of teaching post-graduate classes.

EQUIP. to equip oneself with *furnish*

- You should equip yourself with all the things required on a journey.

ERODE. to erode goodwill *to lose goodwill*

- Public goodwill for the old leader is being eroded daily.

EROTIC. erotic and exotic *romantic and exciting*

- The modern demand is for things both erotic and exotic.

ESCAPE. to make good one's escape *to run away successfully*

- The prisoner made good his escape in the darkness of the night.

to escape from reality *to live in a dream world*

- There is no escape from reality for a married couple.
- Those who try to escape from reality always encounter unhappiness.

ETCHED. to be etched on *engraved deeply*

- Your sound advice is etched on my mind.

EVENING. the evening of life *old age; decline or end of life*

- In the evening of life, one cannot make many new friends.

EXAMINATION. to take an examination *to be examined, to appear for an examination*

- I am taking the IAS examination next year.

EXAMPLE. to set an example *to present a model*

- Teachers should set a right example for students.

EXCEEDING. to an exceeding extent *greatly, overmuch, to excess*

- He drank to an exceeding extent.

EXCEPTION. the exception proves the rule *there is no law which is not violated somewhere; the making of an exception proves that the rule holds in cases not excepted*

- All men are corrupt and exception only proves the rule.

EXEMPT. to exempt from *to free from, not liable to*

- Some brilliant or poor students are exempted from paying fees.
- She was exempted from attending college daily because of her bad health.

EXHIBITIONS. inhibitions and exhibitions *shyness and self-display; humility and boastfulness; self-withdrawal and social spirit.*

- Modern youth are characterised by inhibitions and exhibitions.

EXILE. to send into exile *to banish*

- The king sent the minister into exile.

to go into exile *to go away from home voluntarily*

- When one cannot face the world, one should go into exile.

EXTINCT. to become extinct *to die out*

- Many ancient animals have become extinct today.
- More and more species of flora and fauna will become extinct soon.

EXPENSE. at someone's expense *at someone's cost*

- Don't make a joke at my expense.

EXTREMEST. at the extremest *in the ultimate resort; at the utmost point or verge*

- At the extremest, one may just die.

EXTREMITY. at the last extremity of *on the last point of*

- I found him at the last extremity of life.

EYE. the apple of one's eye *one very dearly loved, something especially dear*

- Kiron is the apple of his mother's eye.

an eye for an eye *equal or matching action*

- The law does not prescribe the principle of an eye for an eye.

F

FACE. face to face *opposite each other*

- The Greek and Persian armies stood face to face in the battle of Thermopylae.

face-lift *beautification of face usually by plastic surgery; improvement of external appearance (extended meaning)*

- She paid her way to America for a face-lift.

- When some foreign head of state arrives, Connaught Place receives a face-lift.

face value *outward appearance; the value shown on the coin or printed on a share certificate, currency note, etc.*

- Everybody has his face value which determines his career in the world.
- The face value of the share was Rs. 100.

FADE. to fade away *disappear*

- Indelible ink gradually fades away with time.

FAIL. to fail in one's expectations *not to be up to the mark*

- The boy failed in his mother's expectations.

FAILURE. conspicuous by one's or their failures *more failures than successes*

Her career is conspicuous by its failures.

FAIR. by fair means or foul *by hook or by crook; anyhow*

- People seek success by fair means or foul.

fair play *honest dealing, just treatment, justice*

- There is no fair play in the business world today.

fair trade *free trade conditional on reciprocity*

- There is no fair trade in the modern world.
- Fair trade was the basis for many businesses to build themselves upon.

FAITH. matter of faith *trust*

- Success in business is a matter of faith for most people, still.

FALL. to fall from grace *to fall into disfavour*

- It is easier to fall from the grace of a VIP than to rise in it.

to fall in line *to go with the majority; conformity*

- Politicians tend to fall in line in order to please the electorate.

to fall in with *to agree*

- The pupils had to fall in with the teacher's views on education.

to fall out *to fight*

- The thieves soon fell out with one another when the question of distribution of the booty arose.

to fall on one's knees *to accept defeat/guilt*

- The prisoner fell on his knees before the judge who had condemned him to death.

FALSE. to play false *to be untrue, to be faithless*

- That woman played false with her trusting husband.

FALLOW. to lie fallow *to be uncultivated*

- Millions of acres of land lie fallow, even today.

FANCY. to take a fancy to *to fall in love with*

- The lady took a fancy to the smart young heir to a sprawling estate in Pachmarhi.

FAR. by far *to a very great degree*

- He is, by far, the best boy in the class.

far and away *very far ahead, by a great deal*

- Delhi is far and away a better place than many small towns.
- She is, far and away, the most beautiful girl in town.

FASHION. in fashion *popular*

- Pizzas are very much in fashion nowadays.

FAT. to live off the fat of the land *to enjoy the best products of the country*

- The affluent classes live off the fat of the land while the poor still struggle to survive.

FATE. to leave one to his fate *to leave uncared for and neglected*

- When Noor Jahan was born, she was left to her fate by her parents on their trek to India.

FAULT. fault-finding *fighting, criticising, quarrelling, finding fault with*

- Fault-finding is a poor profession. As Byron said: "Find some other trade, save censure, for critics are all readymade."

FAUNA. fauna and flora *the assemblage of animals and of vegetable species of a region or period*

- The fauna and flora make the mountains fascinating.

FEAST. feast of fun *sumptuous gratification*

- Puja is a feast of fun in Bengal, like Christmas.

FEATHER. birds of a feather *belonging to the same tribe, ideology, etc.*

- Most politicians, in the final analysis, are birds of a feather, no matter what party they belong to.

make the feathers fly *to throw into confusion by a sudden attack*

- The Vietnamese guerrillas made the Americans' feathers fly.

to feather one's nest *to accumulate wealth for oneself while serving others in a position of trust, to seek one's personal advantage*

- More and more men in the world today are busy feathering their nests rather than working sincerely.

FELINE. feline complex *cat-like ideas*

- Many members of the weaker sex suffer from a strong feline complex.

FELLOW. fine fellow-feeling *fraternity, sympathy, feeling of common interest*

- Seminars are characterised by fine fellow-feeling among the participants.

FELO DE SE. felo de se *self-murder, self-murderer, a suicide, felon of himself*

- The court found the ambassador to be a *felo de se.*
- Frustration sometimes leads to a *felo de se.*

FENCE. to sit on the fence *to join neither side, to be undecided*

- Independent politicians sit on the fence and reap the maximum advantages.

FERRET. to ferret out the truth *to find the truth by using third degree methods, to dig for hidden facts*

- The police torture their suspects to ferret out the truth.

FERTILE. fertile brain *an inventive person, one expert in making schemes or plans*

- Cassius had a fertile brain, full of wiles.

FETTLE. to be in fine fettle *excellent condition*

- Her grandfather is still in fine fettle at 90.
- The prime minister is in fine fettle.

FEVERED. fevered imagination *restless, excited*

- The modern generation's fevered imagination often leads them into trouble.

FIELD. field day *any day of unusual bustle or activity*

- The little boy had a field day today when his school declared a holiday.

field-night *great occasion, a night marked by some important gathering, discussion, etc.*

- August Fifteenth was a field-night for Indians when they gained freedom from British rulers in 1947.

field events *sports other than races (track events)*

- The field events shall be held on Tuesday.

FIG. fig leaf *device for concealing what is indecorous; any scanty clothing*

- Consensus is a kind of fig leaf to avoid a possible split.
- A fig leaf is itself an admission of guilt.

FIGHT. to fight to the finish *fighting till the end*

- The rebels intend to fight to the finish.

FIGHTING. fighting spirit *aggressiveness*

- It pays the oppressed to demonstrate a fighting spirit.

FIGURE. father figure *one who is fit to be father*

- Mahatma Gandhi was a father figure for the country.

FILE. in single file *one after the other*

- The road to Vaishno Devi is so narrow that the pilgrims have to walk in single file.
- The prisoners were asked to move in single file.

FILL. to have one's fill *to eat to one's satisfaction*

- In a marriage party, anyone can have his fill.

FILMY. filmy eyes *dim vision*

- We can only see the future with filmy eyes.

FILTER. to filter through *pass through*

- Light filtered through the thick foliage in the jungle.

FIRE. to be between two fires *having to choose between two alternatives both distasteful or dangerous; to be caught between two troubles*

- Poor children are often caught between two fires—lack of money and the illiteracy of their parents.

to add fuel to the fire *to incite trouble*

- Many leaders of the opposition add fuel to the fire to harass the government through petty agitations.

to go through fire and water *to go through thick and thin, to bear all kinds of troubles and difficulties*

- The friends went through fire and water together.

FIRST. first things first *arranging things to be done in order of importance; giving proper order of priority to work*

- In war-time, we must do first things first.

FISH. queer fish *a strange companion; a person of odd habits*

- The constituents of the new party are queer fish, to say the least.

to fish in troubled waters *to take advantage of troubled times to further one's own interests*

- Parents should save children from fishing in troubled waters on the college campus.
- No patriot will choose to fish in troubled waters when his country is passing through a time of tribulation.

FIX. in a fix *in a confused state of mind; unable to decide; to be in a dilemma or in a difficult situation*

- People with untrained minds are always in a fix.

FIXATION. a fixation *suffering from some special idea; monomania*

- Some great men have suffered from various fixations.

FLAG. to raise the flag of revolt *to rise in opposition, loathing or repugnance*

- Lenin raised the flag of revolt against the Czar.

to lower the flag *to accept defeat; to relinquish command, etc.*

- Time has not yet come for the rebels to lower the flag.

FLAMES. to fan the flames *to increase excitement, and incite people*

- In political trouble, some people fan the flames of discontent.

FLASH. a flash in the pan *a fitful show of beginning without accomplishing anything (metaphor taken from gold-mining)*

- Her success was not a flash in the pan.

to flash across one's mind *to strike one suddenly*

- In a state of concentration, great ideas flash across the mind of a genius.

flash-point *the temperature at which a liquid gives off enough* *inflammable vapour, etc., to flash, when a light is applied to it; point at which indignation, etc., begins*

- Master Tara Singh's "Pakistan Murdabad" at Lahore in 1947 was a flash-point for the Muslims to kill Hindus and Sikhs.

FLESH. flesh and blood *human nature, one's own kindred*

- The suffering was more than flesh and blood could bear during the civil war in China.
- Betrayal by one's own flesh and blood always hurts more.

FLIGHT. flight of the imagination *fantasy*

- Science fiction is no longer just a flight of the imagination.

FLOOR. on the floor *under heated discussion or controversy*

- Many problems are on the floor of the House at present.

FLOP. to end in a flop *to fail, collapse, end in a fiasco or failure*

- The tight-rope walker's performance ended in a flop.

FLUSH. to flush out *seek carefully and remove*

- The enemies were flushed out from the fort and the town.

FLY. to fly high *to dream great dreams*

- The youth fly high and then experience frustration.

FOAM. foam and froth *anger and resentment*

- After much foam and froth, they came to terms and signed an agreement.

FOCUS. focus of attention *centre of interest*

- Everywhere he went, the film star was the focus of attention.

FOIBLES. faults and foibles *failings*

- Jane Austen portrayed vividly the faults and foibles of the English society of her day.

FOIL. to foil an attempt *to prevent a thing from happening*

- The night watchman foiled the attempt of the burglars to break into the house last night.

FOOD. food for thought *something to make one think and ponder*

- The state of the Republic today provides much food for thought for every citizen of India.

FOOLS. fools rush in where angels fear to tread *people take hasty action without thinking of the consequences*

- He said, "Let's find out the true facts before committing ourselves. Fools rush in where angels fear to tread."

FOREWARNED. forewarned is forearmed *those who have knowledge of coming calamities take steps well in time to meet them*

- The general was forearmed because he was forewarned.

FORFEIT. to forfeit one's life *to die*

- Those who lose the war often forfeit their lives.
- Many patriots are willing to forfeit themselves.

FORGE. to forge ahead *to progress*

- The nation must forge ahead both in peace and in war.

FORWARD. to carry forward *to advance*

- We should carry forward the message of "Country before Self."

FOUL. to play foul *to cheat; to be unfair; to do violence or to commit murder*

- It does not pay to play foul with one's friends.

through fair weather and foul *at all times, in joy and in sorrow, in times of prosperity and distress*

- Friends must stick together through fair weather and foul.

FOUNT. to drink at the fount *to get knowledge, etc.*

- You should drink at the fount of the *Bhagavad Gita.*

FRAME. this mortal frame *human body*

- This mortal frame must perish one day.

FRAUGHT. fraught with danger *dangerous, full of risks*

- Youth is fraught with dangers of all kinds.

FREE. free-for-all *in which everybody is free to participate; free fight without rules*

- It was a free-for-all feast.
- It was a free-for-all.

FRENCH. French leave *to depart without notice or permission, depart suspiciously*

- The students quite often take French leave from classes.

FRESH. fresh fields and pastures new *new (romantic or otherwise) adventures without hindrance*

- Youth are always in search of fresh fields and pastures new.

FRET. to fret and fume *to get irritated*

- It is no use fretting and fuming when something has gone wrong.

FRIDAY. Man Friday *faithful helper (from Robinson Crusoe)*

- Naresh is my Man Friday.

FRIGHT. to take fright *to be frightened*

- When she saw the snake, she took fright.

FRIGID. rigid and frigid *harsh and domineering, stiff and unbending*

- Gone are the days when our mothers-in-law were rigid and frigid.

FRINGE. fringe benefits *special allowances, for transport, accommodation, entertainment, etc.*

- Officers in public undertakings enjoy many fringe benefits.

FRITTER. to fritter away *to lose, to waste*

- Do not fritter away the opportunities you have for a true education.

FRO. to and fro *here and there*

- Why are you walking to and fro?

FROWN. luck frowns upon *to be unlucky, hapless*

- Luck always frowns upon the lazy and the indolent.

luck smiles upon *to be lucky*

- Luck smiled upon him when he got his mother's permission to proceed abroad for higher studies.

FRY. small fry *small, unimportant people*

- After the elections are over, the voters are small fry once again.

out of the frying pan into the fire *out of one evil into another*

- In leaving his home and getting no job abroad, the boy threw himself out of the frying pan into the fire.

FULNESS. in the fulness of time *in due course*

- In the fulness of time, Devika Rani became a great actress.

FURROWS. furrows on the face *wrinkles due to old age or worry*

- Most of the old people bear furrows on their faces.

FUSS. to fuss about *to bustle around doing pretty little or nothing*

- What are you fussing about?

FUSTY. fusty musty *stale and tasteless*

- Political orations are usually fusty musty and boring to sit through.

G

GAB. gift of the gab *power of haranguing; popular oratory*

- Nobody can be a successful politician without the gift of the gab.

GAFF. to blow the gaff *to reveal a secret or a plot, to blab*

- We have heard much about the Baroda Dynamite Plot but nobody has yet blown the gaff.
- Some day, someone will blow the gaff about the Harshad Mehta scam.

GAGE. to gage battle *to pledge oneself to judicial combat*

- Uncle Baghi has gaged battle with his tenants.

GAIN. to gain over *to persuade; to do better than*

- The ruling party has gained over diametrically divergent elements in the political life of our country.

to gain the upper hand *to become dominant*

- The working classes have yet to gain the upper hand in the power politics of the country.

to buy/gain time *to cause delay under pretexts*

- The political parties quite often gain time by making impossible promises.

to gain ground *to make progress*

- The Communists are likely to gain ground in this region because of the utter backwardness of the people.

to gain ground upon *to get nearer to*

- The motor-cycle soon gained ground upon the car.

GALAXY. galaxy of the great *a splendid assemblage of important people*

- A galaxy of the great adorned the high platform of the public audience hall in the Red Fort at Delhi.

GALLERY. to play to the gallery *to do something merely to please the common people*

- No leader can be popular without playing to the gallery at some time or other.

GALLOP. full gallop *full speed*

- The new prime minister must go full gallop to redeem the party's pledges to the people.

GALLOWS. **to have the gallows in one's face** *to have the look of one predestined to be hanged*

- A hardened criminal has the gallows in his face.

GAMBLE. **to gamble away** *to lose in gambling*

- He has gambled away lakhs in the casinos of Paris.

to gamble away opportunities *to throw away opportunities through inaction*

- If you do not appear in the UPSC examination, you will be gambling away your opportunities.

GAME. **the same old game** *routine repeated*

- After manifestoes and elections, it is the same old game.

game and game *one game to each side*

- They played game and game.
- Martina and Monica were game and game halfway through the tournament.

to play a good or a poor game *to be a good or a poor player*

- Ram plays a good game sometimes but Tim plays a poor game quite often.

fair game *a legitimate object of pursuit*

- To make money by hook or by crook is regarded as a fair game nowadays.

to die game *to keep up one's spirits to the last, to meet death resolutely or calmly*

- Shahid Bhagat Singh died game.

GANDER. **what is sauce for the goose is sauce for the gander** *what is good for one person is also good for another person*

- Don't think that husbands need money and wives don't. What is sauce for the goose is sauce for the gander.

GANG. to bring to the gang *to punish a seaman by flogging*

- The rebellious crew were brought to the gang.

GAP. to stand in the gap *to fill a breach*

- Since the loss of his father, the son has stood in the gap.

GASP. one's last gasp *the last attempt to breathe before death*

- Mahatma Gandhi had his last gasp on January 30, 1948.

GATHER. to be gathered to one's fathers, one's people *to be buried along with ancestors.*

- The brave soldier was gathered to his people in the village graveyard.

to gather breath *to gain or recover breath*

- The runner gathered breath before he talked to the leader.

to gather oneself together *to acquire self-composure or self-control*

- You must gather yourself together to win the battle of life.

to gather ground *to gain ground*

- Hitler gathered ground in Russia at a heavy cost.

to gather head *to acquire strength; to swell as a festering sore*

- The clouds were gathering head before the storm.
- Discontent was gathering head in the party.
- The wounds on my toes have gathered head.

Gather ye rose buds while ye may *make the best use of your youth while it lasts*

- Youth must gather their rose buds while they may.

GAUNTLET. to run the gauntlet *to face the challenge; to be exposed to unpleasant remarks or treatment*

- One has to run many a gauntlet before one makes good in life.

to throw down the gauntlet *to throw a challenge*

- The Iron Knight threw down the gauntlet to the monsters.

GENEROUS. **to be generous to a fault** *to be more generous than one need be*

- The young employer was generous to a fault in dealing with his employees.

GENTLEMAN. **gentleman's gentleman** *valet*

- Every rich man has a gentleman's gentleman to look after his personal needs.

gentleman of fortune *pirate*

- Some daring gentlemen of fortune built the British Empire.

gentleman's agreement *an agreement binding in honour but not enforceable in law*

- Many transactions are concluded merely as gentleman's agreements.

GET. **to get away with** *to succeed in what one tries to do; to escape punishment*

- Criminals cannot always get away with looting and murder.

to get the better of *to defeat, to prove superior to; to get the upper hand*

- The younger brother got the better of his elder brother in the dispute over their ancestral property.

to get to blows *to start fighting*

- The criminals got to blows while sharing the booty.

to get done with *to succeed in what one tries to do; to escape punishment*

- Let's get done with our chores and go out for a drive.

to get hold of *to catch*

- The police failed to get hold of the murderer.

to get on *to advance; to grow older*

- How are you getting on in life?

- Many people enjoy seeing their friends' children getting on in life.
- My mother is getting on in years, but is still very active.

to get one's way *to do as one pleases*

- Ram got his way at home during his father's absence.

to get by rote *to cram/to learn up*

- Most of the students of today get their lessons by rote.

get-up *style of production, outside look*

- The get-up of this book is very attractive.

to get the upper hand *to gain control of*

- The Army has once again got the upper hand in Pakistan.

to get wind of *to get information beforehand*

- Ameer Ali managed to get wind of the Army's intention to arrest him.

to get the worst of *to meet with a very bad fate; to be the loser*

- The Nazis and Fascists got the worst of the Second World War.

GEWGAW. gewgaw *a gaudy trifle; a toy or bauble*

- Children love gewgaws.

GIFT. do not look a gift horse in the mouth *do not criticise something given free to you*

- Even if one receives **a** fountain pen on one's wedding anniversary, one must not look a gift horse in the mouth.

GINGER. to ginger up *to put pep into; send spirits up*

- The award of a prize gingered up the runner's spirits and he won two more events that day.

GIRD. to gird up one's loins *to prepare for energetic action, as if by tucking up one's clothes; to determine to do*

- The patriots girded up their loins for a fight with the dictatorial government and win the war.

GIRDLE. the girdle of the world *the equator*

- The sun is hottest at the girdle of the world.

to put a girdle round *to go round*

- You can put a girdle round the world in two days.

GIVE. to give the world one's ears *to hear what others have to say*

- Give the world your ears but not your tongue. (Hear what others have to say but say nothing yourself.)

give-and-take *fair exchange*

- We make progress by give-and-take.
- There must be proper give-and-take in a relationship.

to give tongue to *to utter; to speak*

- Please give tongue to your ideas.

to give up *leave; abandon*

- They gave up the attempt to reach the mountain top because of bad weather.
- I have decided to give up smoking.

to give up the ghost *to die*

- Millions gave up the ghost in their country's war of liberation.

to give another (or someone) a piece of one's mind *to take someone to task; to lose one's temper with someone*

- The principal gave the boy a piece of his mind for his misbehaviour in the classroom.
- I gave the maid a piece of my mind when she broke the vase.

GLANCE. at a glance *at one sight; in brief at a stretch, all at once*

- This book gives you much general knowledge at a glance.

GLASS. to live in a glass house *to be unsafe, to be vulnerable, to be open to attack or retort*

- Politicians often feel they are living in a glass house.

- Those who live in glass houses must not throw stones at others.

GLOAT. **to gloat over** *to feast one's eyes upon; to dwell upon with unholy joy*

- Let us not gloat over the misfortunes of our enemies.

GLOVE. **to take up the glove** *to accept challenge, to fight*

- He took up the glove to fight the contender for his beloved's hand.

to throw down the glove (gauntlet) *to offer a challenge to fight*

- The Red Cross Knight threw down the glove to defend the Fairy Queen.

hand-in-glove *on very intimate terms, in close cooperation/ collaboration (usually in nefarions activities)*

- Ram and Sham are hand-in-glove in building up their shady import business.

to fit like a glove *to suit perfectly*

- You fit into this job like a glove.
- The description fits you like a glove.

GO. **to go bang, crash, smash, snap** *to fail*

- All his plans have gone bang, crash, smash, snap.

that goes without saying *that which is a matter of course, what is evident*

- It goes without saying that the rebels and infiltrators must be given no quarter.

to go one's own way *to do according to one's sweet will*

- If you do not take my advice, you may go your own way.

from the word "go" *from the start*

- She was popular at school from the word "go".
- He was successful in business from the word "go".

to go the way of all flesh *to die*

- Everything earthly must go the way of all flesh.

to go to sea *to become a sailor*

- Many folk in our village have gone to sea.

to go to the length of *to go to the limit of*

- Manohar has gone to the length of becoming a paratrooper.

to go a-begging *something which nobody wants*

- The presidentship of this club is going a-begging.
- Jobs on the war-front go a-begging.

to go the whole hog *to do a thing thoroughly or completely*

- The general went the whole hog in attacking the civil population.

to go to one's heart *to cause one great sorrow*

- The death of his father has gone to his heart.
- My son's attitude has really gone to my heart.

to go into *study*

- Please go into the matter carefully.

dead and gone *in a swoon; dead drunk; dead, finished*

- Liquor made him seem dead and gone.

far gone *infatuated*

- He was far gone in his affair with the actress.

GOLD. **to strike gold** *to make money*

- He has dug gold in films.

to be a gold-digger *to run after someone with money (usually for women)*

- Her son's fiancee turned out to be a real gold-digger.

GOLDEN. **golden age** *the period in which literature, arts, culture, etc., were at their highest level of excellence*

- The reign of Ashoka the Great was a golden age for India.

GOOD. **as good as one's word** *to do as you say*

- Politicians are seldom as good as their word.

GRAB. **a grab game** *stealing money in a dispute*

- Politics is regarded by some as a grab game.

to be up for grabs *to be taken away by anyone*

- After his death, his estate was up for grabs.

GRACE. **with good grace** *with a show of willingness, in amiable fashion*

- Chhotelal took his defeat with good grace.

by the grace of God *by the kindness or undeserved mercy of God*

- We shall meet next year, by the grace of God.
- My son has prospered, by the grace of God.

to fall from grace *to cease to be a favourite*

- The minister has fallen from grace with the president.

to have the grace *to show kindness or consideration*

- Kindly have the grace to come home in time.

act of grace *a formal pardon*

- The prisoners were released through an act of grace.

GRADE. **to make the grade** *to show progress, to stand the test, to be up to standard*

- Some new players made the grade in the last Olympics.
- He couldn't make the grade in the entrance test.

GRAIN. **with a grain (or pinch) of salt** *with caution*

- The pledges of a politician should always be taken with a grain of salt.

GRANT. **to take for granted (or someone)** *to regard as not requiring proof, to assume*

- It can be taken for granted that the aggressors will be driven out from Vietnam before long.
- Children often take their parents for granted.

GRASP. **beyond one's grasp** *beyond one's capacity, power*

- Knowledge of death is beyond my grasp as yet.

GRASS. not to let the grass grow under one's feet *not to waste time*

- If you want to pass the UPSC examination, do not let the grass grow under your feet.

to cut the grass from under a person's feet *to thwart; to trip anyone up*

- Mrs. Indira Gandhi hoped to be the Prime Minister in 1977, but the voters of Rae Bareilly cut the grass from under her feet.

GREASE. to grease someone's palm *to bribe*

- You can get nothing done today without greasing somebody's palm.

GREEN. to have green fingers *to be a naturally good gardener*

- My sister has green fingers and her garden is something to behold.

GROUND. to go above the ground *to be proud*

- If you have done something distinctive, learn not to go above the ground.

GUN. a great gun *an important person*

- Ramesh is a great gun today, having become the general manager of his firm.

to be going great guns *to be doing very well at something*

- The Rajiv Gandhi Cabinet was really going great guns for sometime.

H

HABEAS. habeas corpus *a writ to a jailor to produce a prisoner in person and to state the grounds of his detention*

- The prisoner was brought to court because of a *habeas corpus* filed by his father.

HACKLES. to show one's hackles *to show willingness to fight*

- When the police caught the thief, he showed his hackles.

HACKNEYED. hackneyed idiom *an idiom made commonplace by constant and indiscriminate use*

- Avoid hackneyed idioms and phrases because these have lost their effectiveness.

HAIL. within hail (hailing distance) *from where one can be called easily within earshot*

- It is the duty of a personal servant to remain within hail.

out of hail *where a shout cannot reach*

- When she looked for the maid, she was out of hail.

hail fellow, well met *a person on most intimate terms*

- Ram and Sham are hail fellow, well met in their attitude to each other.

HAIR. grey hair *old people*

- There is not much energy left in grey hair.
- Grey hair must be given its due respect.

of one hair *of one colour and external quality*

- These three blankets are of one hair.

to a hair *to a nicety, with complete exactness*

- He copied the portrait to a hair.

to split hairs *to make superfine distinctions*

- You cannot reform the youth by splitting hairs every time you find something wrong in the house.

to keep one's hair on *to keep cool*

- If something goes wrong. please keep your hair on.

not to turn a hair *not to show any sign of being ruffled*

- It is a common quality in a great man not to turn a hair when there is commotion around him.
- Despite the severe storm, the pilot did not turn a hair.

hair's breadth (hairbreadth) escape *narrow escape*

- When the bus fell into the stream, she had a hair's breadth escape.

HALCYON. **halcyon days** *days of calm and peace*

- Old men in modern cities have few halcyon days to experience.
- We all look back to the halycon days of our youth.

HALF. **not half good (or bad)** *not even half, from the due amount*

- Your payment is not half good (or bad) yet.

half-and-half *a mixture of two things in equal proportion*

- Give me half-and-half rose milk.

half-seas-over *half drunk, hal fway across the sea*

- When the secretary came to take the minister home, he found him half-seas-over.

HALL. **A hall! A hall!** *a cry at a mosque, to make room for a dance or important function; also to call people together*

- When the princess came, the bodyguard shouted, "A hall! A hall!"

HALVES. **to go halves** *to divide equally*

- When we won the international prize from the Arab League, Faqir and I went halves.

by halves *half-heartedly*

- You will be frustrated in life if you work by halves.
- You cannot achieve success if you do things by halves.

to cry halves *to claim half a share in something found by another*

- When the man got his bonus, his wife cried halves.

HAMMER. hammer-and-tongs *with great noise and violence*

- The rival parties fought the general elections hammer-and-tongs.
- The couple were always fighting hammer-and-tongs.

HAMSHACKLE. hamshackle ramshackle *restraint through disorder*

- Democracy suffers through hamshackle ramshackle.

HAND. in hand *readily available*

- I have a thousand rupees in hand.

on hand, also at hand *near/approaching*

- Great events are on hand.

to play into the hands of somebody *to serve the purpose of another*

- By ordering elections, the king played into the hands of the opposition.

at the hands of *from the hands of*

- We all suffer at the hands of our enemies.

by hand *by manual action/in person*

- This letter should be delivered by hand.
- Most of the mechanical repairs are done by hand.

off one's hands *out of control*

- I will never let Ritu go off my hands.
- Once my daughter is married, she'll be off my hands.

under the hand of *under the signature of*

- Martial law was declared under the hand of the President.

hand over hand *by passing the hands alternatively one before or above another, as in climbing a rope*

- The students go up the ladder of life hand over hand.

to live from hand to mouth *poorly, improvidently, thriftlessly*

- Millions in the Third World live from hand to mouth.

HANDY. **handy dandy** *fop*

- Modern education tends to make handy-dandies of our children.

HANG. **to get the hang of** *to understand*

- I do not get the hang of what you are saying.

to hang a jury *to prevent a jury from reaching a verdict*

- The accomplices of the criminal hung the jury with their conflicting statements.

to hang up one's sword, gun, etc. *to stop fighting*

- At last the tribals hung up their swords.

HANKER. **to hanker after** *to expect with longing, to long for*

- Modern men hanker after luxuries that are unearned and undeserved.
- Housewives hanker for a rest as much as working women do.

HANKY. **hanky-panky** *trickery; double dealing; underhand dealing*

- Many students get their degrees through hanky-panky.

HAPPY. **happy-go-lucky** *easy-going person*

- School students are usually happy-go-lucky.
- Most people are happy-go-lucky in their youth.

HARD. **hard cash** *money*

- He had to pay Rs. 5000 in hard cash.

hard-favoured *ugly, hard, coarse, forbidding features*

- Most successful criminals are hard-favoured.

to go hard with *turn out ill for*

- It went hard with her when her mother died.

HARMONY. **in harmony with** *in full agreement with*

- The staff must work in harmony with the principal for the betterment of the students.

HARP. to harp upon *to dwell upon a subject tediously*

- There is no use harping upon your success in the examination all the time.

HARRY. Old Harry *a familiar name for the devil*

- You have to make a choice between God and Old Harry in all your dealings in life.

to play Old Harry with *to bedevil; to ruin*

- Misfortunes have played Old Harry with him all his life.

HARVEST. to reap the harvest *to get the reward*

- Work hard and wait patiently to reap the harvest.
- Children often reap the harvest of their parents' efforts.

HASTE. haste makes waste *good results are spoiled through excessive hurry*

- Go slow in your projects, for haste makes waste.

hasten slowly *slow and steady*

- For full success in modern industrialism, you should hasten slowly.

hasty-pudding *flour stirred in milk or water; a temporary measure*

- The achievements of industrialism are hasty-pudding.

HAVE. to have the better of *to defeat; to humble, to score over*

- The Workers' Party had the better of the Conservative Party in the recent elections.

to have to do *to be responsible for*

- The Government has much to do with blackmarketing and general corruption.
- I want to have nothing to do with my wayward son.

HAY. **to make hay while the sun shines** *to seize an opportunity while it lasts*

- The ministers made hay while the sun shone.

HEAD. **to come to a head** *to reach a climax*

- The labours of the government are yet to come to a head.
- Matters came to a head when the rival groups confronted each other.

to head for *to advance*

- The terrible overpopulation is heading for disaster for the world.

head-on *with the head pointing directly at something*

- The cars collided head-on.

to bear or keep head against *to hold one's own against*

- The opposition had to keep head against the party in power.

on one's head *because of*

- The victory of the Janata Party was on Jayaprakash Narayan's head.

over head and ears *completely overwhelmed, deeply submerged or engrossed*

- My father was over head and ears in his work.

head over heels (to fall) *upside down (usually in love)*

- He fell into the pond head over heels.
- He fell head over heels in love with her in college.

to keep one's head *to keep one's wits about oneself.*

- If something goes wrong, keep your head.

by head and shoulders *by force, violently*

- The tenant was ousted by head and shoulders.

to be head and shoulders above *to be much better than others*

- He was head and shoulders above the rest of his colleagues.

from head to toe *completely*

- The soldier was armed from head to toe.
- The rain drenched her from head to toe.

to make head or tail of *to understand, to decipher*

- I cannot make either head or tail of this letter.

to lose one's head *to lose one's temper*

- If you spoil something, do not lose your head.

to keep one's head above water *to be free from debt*

- For the peace of your mind, it is important to keep your head above water.

to take something into one's head *to conceive the idea*

- The tramp took it into his head to rob unwary wayfarers.
- The little boy took it into his head to catch beetles.

to let one have his head *to let one go free*

- The king let the prisoner have his head.
- The cowboy let his horse have his head.

to lay heads together *to consult one another*

- The leaders must lay their heads together to rid the country of the evils of rising prices and corruption.

to talk one's head off *to talk until one is too weary to reply*

- Members of Parliament quite often talk their heads off.

two heads are better than one *two men can think out more correctly than one man singly*

- The king and his minister should put their heads together because two heads are better than one.

HEALTH. **to drink to the health of** *to drink for the well-being of*

- The ministers drank to the health of the king.
- The guests drank to the health of the bride and groom.

HEAP. **all of a heap** *all in a mass*

- The dead soldier lay all of a heap.

to strike all of a heap *to paralyse; to confound utterly*

- The leader's sudden death struck the ministers all of a heap.

HEART. **after one's own heart** *as one desires*

- People have changed governments but they have not yet got the government after their own heart.
- He is a man after my own heart—fun-loving and carefree.

to win the hearts of *to conquer*

- Queen Josephine won the hearts of her people.

to lose heart *to feel disappointed, discouraged*

- If you fail in the examination, do not lose heart. Try harder next time.

nearest to one's heart *closest to one's affections*

- Money-making is nearest to everyone's heart but truth is the farthest off.

to put one's heart into *to be devoted to*

- A student should put his heart into his studies.
- I always put my whole heart into my work, and let God take care of the rest.

with one's whole heart or from the bottom of one's heart *with great sincerity*

- I thank you with my whole heart.

to break the heart of *disappoint*

- A teacher should not break the hearts of his poor students.

to have at heart *to cherish as a matter of deep interest*

- Rosie really desires to get into the Indian Foreign Service at heart.
- I have your best interests at heart.

to lay to heart *to store in the mind for future guidance, to be deeply moved by something*

- The leaders should lay the national problems to heart.

to take to heart *to take seriously*

- He took the death of his friend very much to heart.

to eat one's heart out *to suffer or pine away from vexation*

- The prisoners in jail ate their hearts out for their homes.

to have the heart *to have the courage*

- A cat has the heart to face a dog in defence of her kittens.
- 1 don't have the heart to give her the bad news.

in one's heart of hearts *in one's inmost feelings*

- The leaders of the two parties are alike in their heart of hearts.

heart-to-heart *to talk with frankness and sincerity*

- The father and son talked over the problems heart-to-heart.
- The two sisters had a long heart-to-heart talk when they met.

to have one's heart in one's boots *to be deeply dejected or frightened*

- When the police arrested the high-ranking official, he had his heart in his boots.

heart and soul *the whole of one's affection and energy*

- A worker should put his heart and soul into his work.

to wear one's heart upon one's sleeve *to show one's feelings openly*

- The disappointed suitor should not wear his heart upon his sleeve.
- It doesn't help to wear your heart on your sleeve.

HEAT. to take the heat off *to rob of enthusiasm*

- A cold look from the teacher took the heat off the students.

HEAVE. to heave a sigh *to feel sorry*

- She heaved a sigh for her dead lover.

to heave a sigh of relief *to express relief*

- When the crisis was over, everyone heaved a sigh of relief.

HEAVEN. **to move heaven and earth** *to do one's best*

- The doctor moved heaven and earth to save the child.

HEED. **to pay heed to** *be attentive, attend to*

- Pay heed to what your father says.

to take heed *take care*

- Take heed lest you catch malaria.

HEELS. **to kick one's heels** *to wait idly and impatiently*

- The ministers kicked their heels to meet the C.M.
- The officer kept us all kicking our heels.

to lay by the heels *to arrest, to fetter*

- The criminal was laid by the heels.

to turn up a person's heels *to tumble a person down*

- The police turned up the dacoits' heels.

to show a clean pair of heels *to run away, to evade*

- The boys showed a clean pair of heels to the police after mugging the old lady.

HELL. **hell of a trouble** *very difficult*

- It was hell of a trouble to get the flood victims out and rescue them.

from heaven to hell *from comfort to trouble*

- Her leaving home and going abroad was a transition from heaven to hell.

HELP. **to help oneself to** *to steal; to eat*

- He helped himself to whatever he could find in the house.

HERD. **herd instinct** *following the crowd without thinking*

- The herd instinct prevails on the college campus.

HEYDAY. **heyday** *time of glory or joy*

- 1947 was the heyday for the Indian National Congress.

HIDE. **hide-and-seek** *elusive tricks*

- Fortune often plays hide-and-seek with us.

to hide one's head *to take shelter*

- You cannot hide your head behind ignorance of the law.

HIGH. **high water-mark** *highest point of excellence*

- The ruler achieved the highest water-mark during the war.

HINGE. **to hinge upon** *to depend upon*

- One's success hinges upon both luck and hard work.

HINT. **to hint at** *to make a slight but intelligible suggestion*

- The party president has hinted at action against hoarders and blackmarketeers.

HIT. **to hit upon** *to think out in a flash*

- The general hit upon a plan to rout the enemy.
- The creative director hit upon something really dramatic.

HOARSE. **to cry oneself hoarse** *to shout till one can shout no more*

- The poor people are crying themselves hoarse against rising prices.

HOBNOB. **hobnob** *to drink together*

- He hobnobs with drunkards and gamblers.
- Don't hobnob with people from a different class of society.

HODGEPODGE. **hodgepodge** *a clumsy mixture of ingredients*

- The men in the mob are a hodgepodge.

HOG. **to go the whole hog** *to do a thing thoroughly*

- Sarla went the whole hog to find the right bride for Raju.
- When having a party for her son, she decided to go the whole hog.

HOLD. **hold-up** *highway dacoity*

- He lost all his possessions in a hold-up.

HOLE. **to pick a hole in something** *to find faults*

- Don't pick a hole in your well-wishers' suggestions.
- The Opposition picked holes in the Government's proposed Bill.

hole and corner *secret, clandestine, underhand*

- The revolutionary soldiers are said to have used hole and corner methods to collect funds for their campaigns.

HOLLOW. **to render hollow** *to prove false; to empty out*

- The woodpeckers rendered the tree-trunk hollow.
- Their success was rendered hollow by the price they had to pay for it.

a hollow victory *to win after a heavy price*

- The Congress had a hollow victory in the last elections after Rajiv Gandhi's death.

HOME. **a home away from home** *a home in a new place which provides homelike accommodation and amenities*

- Indians in Indonesia have found a home away from home.

at home *fully at ease*

- Please feel at home when you come to our house, even if we are not in.

nearer home *near one's dwelling place or country*

- India has found a gold mine nearer home, in the Middle East.

HONEST. **honest to God** *honest, even if nobody is watching one's actions*

- Few men today are honest to God.

HONEYED. **with a honeyed tongue** *using honeyed words; flattering*

- She spoke to the crowd with a honeyed tongue.

HOOK. **by hook or by crook** *anyhow; by fair means or foul*

- The craze for money is spreading and people want to get rich quickly by hook or by crook.
- Most young men want to get on by hook or by crook.

HOOPS. with hoops of steel *firmly*

- "Hold fast to sincere friends with hoops of steel," said Shakespeare in *Hamlet.*

HOPE. to hope against hope *to hope in spite of all grounds having gone*

- She hoped against hope that her mother would survive her serious illness.
- She hoped against hope that her friend would recover her lost jewellery.

HORIZON. beyond the horizon *far beyond where the eye can reach*

- While we struggle for immediate advantages, human welfare lies beyond the horizon.

HORN. to blow one's own horn *to boast*

- During the elections, every political party blows its own horn.
- These days, it is almost necessary to blow one's own horn in order to make a mark.

to lift up the horn *to exalt oneself; to show fight*

- When a person has health and wealth, he is in a position to lift up the horn.

the horn of plenty *cornucopia; the horn of plenty is a symbol of peace and prosperity*

- We are waiting for the horn of plenty from our rulers.

to put to the horn *to proclaim an outlaw by three blasts of the horn*

- During World War II, many patriots were put to the horn.

HORNET. (to stir up) a hornet's nest *a place of trouble*

- The tanks created a hornet's nest for the invaders.
- In fighting the mobsters, they had stirred up a hornet's nest.

to bring a hornet's nest about one's ears *to stir up a host of enemies round oneself*

- The loud noise and bustle of their quarrel brought the hornet's nest about the dacoits' ears.

HORSE. to talk horse *to talk big or boastfully*

- When poor people do well in life, they talk horse.

to work for a dead horse *to work for what has been paid in advance and so brings in no advantage*

- When you take all the payment in advance, it is hard to work for a dead horse.

to flog a dead horse *to engage in fruitless effort*

- To try to revive the dead man is to flog a dead horse.

horse and foot *with all one's might (origin: with cavalry and infantry)*

- They fought horse and foot to win the war.

horse-play *rough, coarse and boisterous play*

- The students indulged in horse-play in the class as the teacher was away.

HOT. to blow hot and cold *to talk incongruently, to be favourable and unfavourable by turns*

- The politicians blow hot and cold except during elections.

to make it too hot for *to make the position uncomfortable*

- The police made it too hot for the dacoits to operate in the city.
- The smuggler found it too hot to face the customs official at the airport.

too hot to hold *too disagreeable to manage*

- He found the job as administrator in the college campus too hot to hold.

hot-bed *a place favourable to rapid growth*

- Trade and politics have always been hot-beds of intrigue.

HOTCHPOTCH. hotchpotch *hodgepodge, clumsy mixture, a confused mass of ingredients*

- The training programme was a hotchpotch and nobody benefitted from it.

HOUND. to hound out *to drive out*

- The rebels were hounded out of the country.
- The honest clerk was hounded out by his corrupt colleagues.

to run with the hare and hunt with the hounds *to play a double game; to double-cross; to betray both sides*

- Some political workers run with the hare and hunt with the hounds.

HOUSE. to make a house *to build up a family*

- The married couple set about to make a house soon.

to keep house *to look after household affairs*

- When the wife goes to work, how can she keep house alone without any help from the husband?

house of ill-fame *a brothel*

- Many youngsters visit houses of ill-fame.

like a house on fire *in great agitation, with astonishing rapidity*

- Between her husband and her lover, she felt like a house on fire.
- They get on together like a house on fire.

to break into the house *to steal things, to force an entry into a house*

- The thieves broke into the house in my absence.

HOVER. **to hover over** *to keep hanging around*

- The flies hover over sweetmeats.
- The hostess hovered over the table, checking everything out.

HUB. **hub-a-dub** *the noise of beating a drum*

- An Indian marriage is characterized by much hub-a-dub.

HUBBLE. **hubble-bubble** *confusion; a crude kind of* hookah

- Old village folk are fond of the hubble-bubble.

HUE. **hue and cry** *clamour*

- There was much hue and cry when a pickpocket was caught.

HUFF. **in a huff** *to mind something; acting in anger*

- When the banks were nationalized, the minister resigned in a huff.

HUNGER. **hunger-bitten** *pinched with hunger, starving*

- More and more educated unemployed are hunger-bitten.

HUNT. **to hunt after** *to seek; to pursue*

- Boys hunt after girls both on the campus and off it.

HURDY. **hurdy-gurdy** *a fat awkward person, a stringed instrument, like a crude violin; a water wheel driven by a jet of water under pressure*

- Hurdy-gurdies eat a lot at mealtimes.
- The hurdy-gurdy is a popular item at village fairs.

HURRICANE. **a hurricane tour** *a swift tempestuous campaign*

- The party office-bearers made many hurricane tours of India during the elections.

HURRIED. **hurried and worried** *anxious*

- Many men today lead hurried and worried lives.

HURRY. **hurry-scurry** *in a disorderly haste,pellmell, confusion and bustle*

- When the air raid siren was sounded, people left the hall in a hurry-scurry.

HUSH. **hush-hush** *secret; especially of an armament designed to take an enemy by surprise*

- The invention of the atom bomb in 1945 was a hush-hush weapon in the Allied armoury.

hush money *money paid to hush up a crime*

- The murderer paid hush money to the police but it did not save his neck.

HUSK. **to take the grain and throw away the husk** *to avail oneself of important things and let the unimportant ones go; make the best use of life*

- The discipline of education should teach a man to take the grain and throw away the husk.

HUSTLE. **hustle-bustle** *commotion, uproar*

- There is much hustle-bustle in a marriage.
- The growing hustle-bustle of life today taxes our nerves tremendously.

HYDRA. **hydra-headed** *having many heads, many manifestations*

- Corruption is a hydra-headed monster.

I

I. **"I" and "My"** *ego*

- "I" and "my" are at the root of all trouble.

another I *second self; a manifestation of powerfrom something which is not I (Carlyle)*

- Above the I of a man, there is another I.
- My friend is another I.

ICY. icy hands *the hands of death*

- Death lays its icy hands on kings and paupers alike.

IDÉE FIXE idée fixe *a fixed idea*

- Every great man has an idée fixe.

IDLE. to idle away *to waste*

- Don't idle away your youth.
- Don't idle away your vacation, learn something useful instead.

ILL. to take (something) ill *to mind*

- Please don't take it ill if I tell you to go home now.

It's an ill wind that blows nobody any good *something that is of benefit to nobody*

- Crime is an ill wind that blows nobody any good.

ill at ease *perturbed*

- A grocer is always ill at ease lest his provisions run out.

to speak ill of *censure, to criticise*

- Don't speak ill of your friends.

ill-off (badly off) *not well-off, in bad circumstances*

- Many people are ill-off due to rising prices.

as ill-luck would have it *because of bad luck*

- As ill-luck would have it, I lost all my money.
- It's my ill-luck that the storm destroyed the crops.

ill-will *unkind feeling, animosity*

- What is the use of doing something that brings you only ill-will?

IMPETUS. to lose the impetus *to lose enthusiasm*

- We should never lose the impetus to do the right thing at all times.

IMPROMPTU. impromptu *without preparation; off-hand*

- The headman spoke impromptu.
- The children put on an impromptu show on the weekend.

IMPULSE. **to lose the impulse** *to lose the initiative*

- A political party should not lose the impulse after winning elections.

IN. **ins and outs** *secrets*

- A minister should study the ins and outs of his portfolio.

in it, win it *whatever you undertake, do it successfully*

- Since you are in it, you must win it.

in bed *sleeping*

- Madame is still in bed.
- Andrew stays in bed late on holidays.

in a blaze *enjoying publicity*

- Every actress is in a blaze.

in chains *under arrest*

- The murderer is in chains.

in debt *indebted*

- Poor labourers are always in debt.

in fine *in short*

- In fine, he is a great actor.

in school *studying, getting educated*

- My boy is still in school.

INCH. **inch by inch** *slowly*

- They marched forward inch by inch.

INFEST. **infested with** *full of*

- The house is infested with mosquitoes.

INFLAME. **to be inflamed with** *to burn with*

- He was inflamed with indignation.

INFUSE. **infuse with** *energise*

- He infused the soldiers with patriotism.

INJECT. inject with *infuse with*

- He injected the youth with courage and daring.

IRONS. to have too many irons in the fire *too many things on hand at once*

- Mohan has too many irons in the fire; hence he cannot concentrate on anyone.

J

JACK. Jack of all trades *one who can turn his hand to anything*

- Indian mechanics are greatly in demand in the Middle East because they are Jacks of all trades.
- He is a Jack of all trades and master of none, and never tries to specialise.

JADED. jaded and faded *tired out*

- When a working girl returns home in the evening, she is quite jaded and faded.

JAM. in a jam *in a difficult position*

- He is in a jam because he could not account for the money he had spent on behalf of the society.

a traffic jam *a traffic bottleneck*

- We were held up in a traffic jam for almost an hour last evening.
- Traffic jams are a daily occurrence in some parts of the city.

JAR. to jar on the ears *to be discordant; unpleasant*

- Traffic hoots jar on the ears.

JET. jet set *a sophisticated company of rich people who travel by jet planes as a routine*

- It is the age of the jet set who breakfast in Bombay, lunch in London and take their dinner in New York!

- Everyone with money tries to get into the jet set.

JIFFY. **in a jiffy** *quickly, in a flash*

- Go ahead please, I am following you in a jiffy.

JIM. **Jim Crow** *a generic name for the Negro*

- No South African European should talk of a Jim Crow.

JOCKEY. **to jockey for a position** *to get a position by hook or by crook*

- After elections, members of Parliament jockey for ministerships.

JOINT. **out of joint** *in great disturbance*

- During war, the times are out of joint.

JONATHAN. **Brother Jonathan** *personified American people collectively; a typical specimen*

- If a highwayman holds you up, do not depend on Brother Jonathan.

JOVE. **by Jove** *by God*

- By Jove, I will not let you down in your hour of trial and tribulation.

JOWL. **cheek by jowl** *side by side*

- Children walk to school cheek by jowl.

JOY. **joy ride** *ride for pleasure*

- Some teenagers often go on joy rides.

JUDGE. **judge not that ye be not judged** *do not criticise others, so that others may not criticise you*

- Jesus Christ said to his followers, "Judge not that ye be not judged."

JUMP. **to jump to conclusions** *to draw an inference prematurely without proper thought*

- Do not jump to conclusions that everything will be rosy for • you in the future.

K

KALEIDOSCOPE. kaleidoscopic view *picturesque scenery*

- You can get a kaleidoscopic view of Simla from the Monkey Hill.

KEEL. to keel over *to upset; to capsize*

- Shelley's pleasure-boat, the *Ariel,* keeled over in a storm and he was drowned.
- She keeled over suddenly after a strenuous game of tennis.

KEEP. for keeps *for good, permanently*

- This book is yours for keeps.

in good keeping *in good custody, charge*

- The child is in good keeping.

to keep on good terms with *to live in peace with*

- You must keep on good terms with your neighbours.

to keep under *to enslave, hold down in restraint*

- The Europeans kept Asia and Africa under for a hundred years.

to keep down *to prevent from thriving*

- You can't keep a good man down.

KEY. key figure *central figure*

- The Prime Minister is the key figure in a government.
- He was the key figure in the political drama.

key-note *dominant idea, any central principle or controlling thought*

- Democratic liberty is the key-note of a progressive party.

KILL. to kill two birds with one stone *to do wo jobs with a single effort*

- By getting a job, you kill two birds with one stone because you get both economic freedom and money to enjoy yourself.

KISS. Judas-kiss *kiss of deception, any act of treachery under the guise of kindness*

- It was the Judas-kiss that betrayed Jesus Christ into the hands of his tormentors.

KITE. to fly a kite *to imagine; to spread gossip or rumours to see how the wind blows*

- He flew a kite that he was going to be a minister.

KNICK-KNACK. knick-knack *a small, trifling ornamental article; a light article of furniture, dress*

- She loaded the showcase with knick-knacks.
- The room was beautifully decorated but full of too many knick-knacks.

KNOCK. to knock out *to defeat; destroy; kill; eliminate*

- Our cricket team was knocked out at Madras.
- The police knocked out the dacoits in the bloody encounter that followed the chase.

KOWTOW. kowtow *the Chinese custom of touching the ground with the forehead by way of submission, the Chinese ceremony of prostration*

- The people kowtowed to the old emperor.
- One can see hangers-on kowtowing to ministers and men in power.

L

LACED. to be laced round *to surround*

- The Himalayas are laced round by rivers.

LACK. for lack of *for want of*

- He could not pursue higher studies for lack of monetary resources.

LADDER. **up the ladder** *in a higher position*

- Gradually every officer moves up the ladder.

down the ladder *in a lower position*

- For lack of proper study, the boy has gone down the ladder in the examination.

LADY. **lady-killer** *a man who fancies himself irresistible to women, a general lover; a philanderer*

- Lady-killers haunt the college campuses nowadays.

lady-love *a man's sweetheart, a lady or woman loved*

- She was his lady-love.
- Young men are always trying to please their lady-loves.

LAG. **to lag behind** *to be slower than the rest*

- Don't let your son lag behind in the class.

LAID. **to be laid up** *to suffer from*

- The boy was laid up in bed for two days with high fever.

LAME. **lame excuse** *an excuse which is obviously unsatisfac tory or unconvincing*

- If you cannot keep your appointment, don't make a lame excuse.

lame duck *disabled or weak person; a defaulter*

- A picnic cannot succeed with lame ducks.

LAP. **in one's lap** *within one's reach*

- Victory is in your lap.

LAST. **last but not least** *something mentioned last in order but being of equal importance with things mentioned earlier*

- Gandhi was democratic, public-spirited, daring and true. Last but not least, he honoured even his enemies.

LATE. **of late** *recently*

- Foodstuffs have become costlier of late.

at the latest *at the very last moment*

- You must check in at midnight, at the latest, to catch the plane for London.

LAUGH. laughing-stock *an object of general scorn or ridicule*

- A poor student usually becomes the laughing-stock in a public school.

butt of someone's laughter *target of scorn or ridicule*

- The students made the teacher the butt of their laughter.

LAUNCH. to launch upon *start*

- They launched upon the new enterprise with great enthusiasm.

LAURELS. to win laurels *to get honours*

- Prakash Padukone won laurels in badminton many times.

LAY. to lay up *to store*

- "Do not lay up your treasures on this earth," said Jesus Christ, "for the moths will eat them up. Lay up your treasures in heaven."

to lay off *to terminate the services of*

- Thousands of workers have been laid off on account of the management's policy of retrenchment.

to lay (something) down in black and white *to write down, to affirm, assert*

- Please lay down your ideas in black and white.

LEAD. to lead astray *to draw into wrong course; to seduce from right conduct; to misguide*

- The ruffians led the innocent boy astray.

to lead by the nose *to keep under full control*

- Birbal usually led the king by the nose.
- The domineering wife truly led her husband by the nose.

to lead a dog's life *to live miserably*

- Millions in India today lead a dog's life.

to lead up the garden path *to lead one on insensibly; to mislead; to cheat*

- Confidence tricksters lead their victims up the garden path.
- Young men often lead unsuspecting girls up the garden path with promises of marriage.

to lead to the altar *to marry*

- Burt Lancaster led the actress to the altar.

LEAF. to turn over a new leaf *to reform oneself; to begin a new and better course of conduct*

- The older a man grows, the more difficult it is for him to turn over a new leaf.

to take a leaf out of someone's book *to learn from the example of; to profit by another's example*

- Ramesh did not take a leaf out of Sanjay's book.

LEAP. by leaps and bounds *quickly; at a fast pace*

- Politicians gather pelf, power and possessions by leaps and bounds.

LEASE. a fresh lease of life *return to health from near-death*

- After her heart by-pass operation, she got a fresh lease of life.

LEASH. hold in leash *keep tied with a rope, etc; control by a line a hawk, a hound, etc.*

- A ferocious animal must be held in leash.

LEAVEN. to act as leaven upon *to act as anything that makes a general change, to spread agitation or radical ideas*

- The Marxist-Leninist ideology worked as a leaven upon the working class.

LEFT. the left *radical party in politics inclined towards Communism*

- The socialists form the Left Bloc in Indian politics.

LEGEND. to become a legend *to become historically well-known*

- Mahatma Gandhi had become a legend very early in his own lifetime.
- Shahnaz Husain has become a legend in the world of herbal beauty aids.

LEGS. on wooden legs *false, without reality*

- Propaganda alone cannot go far on wooden legs; it must be backed by substance.

LEISURE. at (one's) leisure *in one's free time*

- Please call on me at your leisure.

gentleman of leisure *man without work, well provided for*

- He tried to live the life of a gentleman of leisure after making his money in the stock market.
- Gentlemen of leisure haunt the coffee houses.

LENGTH. at length *at last; ultimately*

- At length, the patient was hospitalised and had to be operated upon.

LESSON. to learn a lesson *to get practical experience and become wise*

- Most people never learn a lesson except through suffering.
- My bad experience with him has made me learn a lesson for future dealings.

LET. to let *to be available for residence on rent; when you don't have money*

- This house is to let.
- My pockets are to let these days.

let up *pause; time for rest*

- There is no let up in the struggle for survival for a poor man.
- The rain didn't let up for hours yesterday.

LETTER. **to the letter** *exactly; perfectly*

- The assassins carried out their plan to the letter.

in spirit rather than the letter *actually and not merely to make a show of it*

- We should obey laws in spirit, and not merely in the letter.

in letter and in spirit *both formally and actually*

- Let us be friends both in letter and in spirit.
- They decided to honour their agreement both in letter and in spirit.

LEVEL. **one's level best** *one's very best*

- Do your level best to pass the IAS examination.

death levels the crown with the sickle and the spade *death makes a king the equal of a labourer, i.e., all men are equal in death*

- When the emperor passed away, death levelled the crown with the sickle and the spade.

LIBERTY. **to set at liberty** *to free*

- They set the prisoner at liberty after five years.

liberty without licence *freedom which does not lead to its abuse.*

- Democracy promises liberty without licence only in theory.

LIEU. **in lieu of** *in place of*

- You may use a pen in lieu of a pencil.

LIFE. **to take one's life** *to kill*

- The robbers took their victim's life.
- No man has the right to take the life of another man.

LIFT. **to give one a lift** *to encourage; to give promotion; to improve chances of success in life*

- Every parent tries to give his children a lift in life.

LIGHT. **to throw light on** *to add further information about*

- Will you please throw some light on your desire to quit this job?

LIGHTNING. at lightning speed *very fast*

- The Indian Army struck back at Pakistan at lightning speed.

LIKING. to one's liking *to one's taste*

- You will find the garden here to your liking.

LIMBO. to cast into limbo *to forget*

- Old friends are cast into limbo.
- Retired employees are often cast into limbo in their old age.

LIMELIGHT. to come into the limelight *to become famous*

- After elections, new leaders have come into the limelight.
- Sushmita Sen really brought India into the limelight in the world of fashion.

LIMIT. to the utmost limit *to the maximum*

- I shall stand by you to the utmost limit.

LINE. in line with *according to*

- Your ideas are in line with my thinking.
- A minister's speech has to be in line with the policies of the government.

to draw a line on *to put a limit on*

- He drew a line on his expenses.

LION. to beard a lion in his own den *to humble an enemy within his own defence*

- The Indian Army bearded the lion in his own den in East Pakistan in 1971.

to make a lion of *to idolise*

- They made a lion of the leader after his victory in the elections.

LIP. to pay lip service to *to make a show of homage*

- Most people pay lip service to people in high places.

- Only lip service is paid to Gandhi's ideology today.

LITTLE. little people *fairies*

- Little people visit children every night.

LIVE. to live by one's wits *to earn one's living by ingenious expedients rather than through honest labour*

- Some artists learn to live by their wits.
- Wheeler-dealers live in the world of business by their wits.

LOCUS. locus standi *place of standing, recognised place or position*

- A new tenant has no locus standi in the colony.
- It took him some time to create a locus standi in the office.

LOLL. to loll about *to hang about; to wander aimlessly*

- Why are you lolling about in the park instead of studying?

LONG. the long and the short of a matter *in brief, the essence, the sum total of the matter in a few words*

- The long and the short of it is that I need money.

(to give someone) the long rope *full scope to defeat one's own ends*

- The police give the criminals a long rope to hang themselves with.

to have long sight *to have foresight; to be sagacious*

- Gandhiji had long sight about the future of India.

LOOK. to look down upon *to hate; to hold cheap; to think badly of*

- Do not look down upon the poor beggars.
- Children from public schools look down upon those from ordinary backgrounds.

to look over *to ignore*

- Do not look over the defects of your children.

to look up to *to respect, to feel veneration for*

- Always look up to your teachers.

LOOM. to loom on the horizon *appear*

- Great prospects loom on the horizon.

LOOSE. to let loose *to free from constraint; untie*

- The dog was let loose after many hours of chaining.
- Don't let children loose in the street.

LORD. to lord it over *to play the lord; to tyrannise*

- You cannot lord it over your children nowadays.

LOSE. to lose one's face *to be humiliated*

- Dishonest people lose face sooner or later, when caught.
- The Japanese prefer to die rather than lose face.

LOSS. at a loss *in a fix; unable to decide*

- I am at a loss to know whether to go home or stay here.

loss, toss or cross *come what may, no matter what*

- I am going to do this work, loss, toss or cross.

LOST. no love lost *there exists no love*

- There is no love lost between the two neighbours.

LOT. bemoan one's lot *to feel sorry for one's misfortunes*

- She was found always bemoaning her lot.
- It does no good to bemoan one's lot. Difficulties have to be overcome.

LOTH. loth to *unwilling; disinclined*

- An educated man is loth to do manual work and so he starves, if he doesn't get the right job.

LULL. a lull before the storm *the weather is quite calm before the storm breaks out; one has a little time of peace before troubles break out on one's head violently*

- If you are complimenting yourself upon your good fortune, do not forget that it might well be a lull before the storm.

- The relationship between India and Pakistan is quiet, but it may be a lull before the storm.

LURCH. **to leave someone in the lurch** *to leave someone in difficulties*

- Children do not leave your friends in the lurch.

LURK. **lurk in the dark** *to move about secretly or unseen; something or someone prowling around unseen*

- Danger always lurks in the dark.
- Children are often frightened of something lurking in the dark.

LUSTRE. **to lose lustre** *to lose popularity*

- After losing an election, a leader usually loses his lustre.
- A film star loses his lustre after a failure at the box office.

LUXURY. **to roll in luxury** *to lead a luxurious life*

- After his business prospered, he was rolling in luxury.
- A few roll in luxury, while millions grovel in the dust.

LYNCH. **lynch-law** *to judge and put to death without the usual forms of law*

- Sooner or later, the hoarders will have to face the lynch-law of the public.

M

MAIDEN. **maiden speech** *first speech*

- He delivered his maiden speech in Parliament yesterday.

MAIN. **with might and main** *with full endeavour, with utmost strength*

- You should work for success with might and main.

MAKE. **to make out** *to understand*

- I cannot make out your letter.

- It's difficult to make out what he is trying to say.

to make one's way *to go ahead*

- You should try to make your way in life.
- I like to see young people making their way in life.

make or mar *build or spoil*

- Youth, if left alone, can make or mar their careers, without proper guidance.

to make up *to beautify with paint and powder; to patch up a quarrel; to compensate*

- The actress was all made up for the evening's performance.
- The lovers decided to make up after their tiff.
- The train driver tried to make up the lost time.

to make one's destiny *to decide one's fate*

- Everybody makes his own destiny.

to make time *to find an opportunity to regain the advantage of lost time*

- He is making the time lost in his recent illness.

MANTLE. to bear the mantle of *to shoulder the responsibilities of*

- The son bears the mantle of his father on his death.

MAP. map out *to plan out, make arrangements for*

- They mapped out the trek to the Himalayas.

MARCH. to march with *to go along with*

- Prices march with demand and supply.

to steal a march on *to gain an advantage over someone unperceived*

- Alexander the Great stole a march upon King Porus.

MARK. to mark time *to wait patiently; to keep things going without progressing*

- The young man is marking time to inherit his father's property.
- He is marking time before the elections.

to mark down *to book for punishment*

- Every ruler marks down his enemies.

mark out *to be destined; to lay out the plan or outlines of*

- Ram is marked out for scholarship.
- He knew that the girl was marked out for success.

to make your mark *to earn a good reputation*

- He has made his mark in his profession.

MARKET. man of the market *shopkeeper*

- It is best to meet a man of the market in the market.

MARROW. to the marrow of his bones *completely*

- He will remain honest to the marrow of his bones.
- He is religious right down to the marrow of his bones.

MARTYR. a martyr to *one who suffers for*

- Every parent is a martyr to his children.

MAST. serve before the mast *to be a sailor*

- It was my ambition early in life to serve before the mast.

MASSE. en masse *as a body; all together*

- People en masse are selfish.
- When a holiday was declared, the children rushed out of the classroom én masse.

MATCH. to match one's wits against *to compete mentally*

- The students match their wits against one another in the group discussions.
- The grand masters matched their wits against each other in the chess tournament.

MATTER. as a matter of fact *in reality; indeed*

- As a matter of fact, the king knows pretty little about his subjects.

a matter of regret *sad affair; something not very good*

- It is a matter of regret that you arrived late for the function

a matter of convenience *for personal comfort*

- Marriage is a matter of mutual convenience.

MEALY. mealy-mouthed *flattering; not outspoken*

- Many men who haunt ministers' bungalows are mealy-mouthed creatures.

MEASURE. measure for measure *equal; match for match*

- Communism and capitalism are measure for measure.

MEDAL. the other side of the medal or coin *the contrary view*

- You should see the other side of the medal (coin) before arriving at your judgement.

MELT. to melt a heart of iron *to get compassion even from a hard-hearted person*

- Her condition was such that it would melt a heart of iron.

MEMORY. as an aid to memory *something to remember by*

- He gave me a ring as an aid to memory.

MERRY. to make merry *to enjoy oneself*

- The kith and kin make merry to celebrate a marriage.

MESS. in a mess *in great confusion*

- When the king died, everything was in a mess.

MILK. the milk of human kindness *humanity; compassion*

- Hoarders and blackmarketeers are without the milk of human kindness.
- One can never have too much of the milk of human kindness.

MILLS. the mills of God grind slowly; but grind exceedingly small *God takes time to punish the evil but he punishes unsparingly*

- The evil-doers must realise that the mills of God grind slowly but they grind exceedingly small.

MILLSTONE. a millstone round one's neck *a heavy responsibility*

- The job of a Prime Minister of a big country is a millstone round the neck of the incumbent.

MINCE. to mince words *to talk daintily; to soften words unduly*

- One who speaks the truth does not mince words.

MIND. to mind your own business *take care of the work entrusted to you*

- Please mind your own business and do not meddle in the affairs of others.

to have in mind *to remember, to plan something*

- Please have in mind what I told you — to start a new project for me.
- I had a new kind of book in mind.

to give someone a bit or piece of one's mind *to take to task*

- A good mother gives her errant child a bit of her mind.

to keep (something or someone) in mind *remember*

- I will always keep you in mind.
- Please keep me in mind when you make fresh appointments.

out of one's mind *insane*

- The woman is out of her mind.

to keep (have) on one's mind *on your mind; to take to heart; to feel sorrow*

- Please do not keep the loss of your pet cat on your mind.
- You are under stress and have too much on your mind.

MINISTER. to minister to one's needs *to cater/to provide for*

- A mother ministers to the needs of her children.

MINT. to mint money *to make money quickly*

- People go abroad to mint money.
- Garment exporters are minting money these days.

MISFORTUNES. misfortunes never come singly but in battalions *troubles come together in crowds*

- The boy lost his father, his mother and his job, too. For him misfortune didn't come singly but in battalions.

MISS. hit or miss *success or failure*

- For every youngster doing well is a hit or miss affair.
- Sometimes hit and miss methods yield results.

to miss the mark *to fail to hit the target*

- He missed the mark at the IAS examination.

MITE. mite or trite *anything very small*

- A starving person is ready to work for mite or trite.

MOCKERY. to make a mockery of *to reduce to a joke or farce*

- The iron-fisted dictator made a mockery of democracy.

MOGHUL. grand Moghul *a great personage*

- Raj Kapoor was a grand Moghul in the film world.

MOMENT. for the moment *for a short time*

- Every minister is a prince for the moment.

from one moment to another *for a very short time*

- A cancer patient enjoys a lease of life from one moment to another.

MOMENTUM. to gain momentum *to quicken the speed of progress*

- India's economic recovery is gaining momentum from year to year.

MONKEY. to make a monkey of *to befool*

- When he was invited to dinner on April 1st, he found that he had only been made a monkey of.

MOOD. the mind, the mood and the moment *general climate or the prevailing situation*

- You must understand the mind, the mood and the moment before you borrow money from somebody.

MOONSHINE. moonshine *visionary stuff; illicitly distilled spirits*

- The romantic poetry of Shelley is all moonshine.
- When he asked for champagne, he was given moonshine.

MORTGAGE. to mortgage one's future *to lose the chances of future progress*

- If you do not work hard and make the most of your opportunities, you are only mortgaging your future.

MOSS. a rolling stone gathers no moss *one who moves from place to place can make no real progress or attachments*

- He would have done well if he had stuck to one job, but a rolling stone gathers no moss.

MOST. to make the most of *to put to best use, to give great importance to*

- I must make the most of the time at my disposal in the examination hall.
- She is not good looking, but knows how to make the most of herself.

at the most *if the worst happens*

- At the most, they can put a debtor in prison for non-payment of a debt.

MOUNT. to mount the losses *to increase losses*

- When Napoleon made a frontal attack, it mounted his losses, but also gave him a tactical advantage.

MOUNTAIN. to make a mountain out of a molehill *to exaggerate troubles*

- I know that you are in financial difficulties and physical trouble; but nevertheless, you must not make a mountain out of a molehill.

MOURN. to mourn the loss of *condole*

- A meeting was held to mourn the loss of a dear friend the other day.
- The older generation mourns the loss of different value systems.

MOUTH. from mouth to mouth *orally*

- News spreads in a village from mouth to mouth.
- Rumours travel from mouth to mouth, and always gain something.

to shut one's mouth *not allow one to speak*

- The boy wanted to say something but his mother shut his mouth.

to make one's mouth water *to arouse a delightful feeling of anticipation or desire (for food)/ to tempt*

- He did not want to go abroad but the opportunities to get rich quickly made his mouth water.
- The beautiful illustrations in the magazine made my mouth water.

from hand to mouth *miserably, in a state of poverty*

- Millions in India live from hand to mouth.
- I am sick of living from hand to mouth and now want to get rich.

MOVE. to make a move *to get going, to do something; to leave*

- It is time to make a move.

without moving a little finger *without any physical exertion*

- A powerful man can get everything done without moving a little finger.

MOW. to mow down *to massacre*

- Chengiz Khan mowed down the people of any city he conquered and made a Tower of Skulls to celebrate his victory.
- The terrorists mowed down the people working in the fields.

MUCH. to make much of *to give great importance to*

- An actress is made much of in society.

MUDDLE. to muddle through *to work in a confused manner*

- Most of the students muddle through their examinations somehow.

MUG. mug up *cram*

- You will learn little if you simply mug up your notes.

MUGGER. hugger-mugger (same as hush-hush) *secrecy, confusion; secret, confused*

- The diplomats prefer to work in a hugger-mugger style.
- It was a hugger-mugger deal between Italy and Germany.

MULTAN. multan in parvo *much in little*

- An atom is *multan in parvo.*

MULTIPLY. to multiply one's troubles *to increase one's troubles*

- Do not multiply your troubles by crying over them.
- Multiply your happiness by laughing at your troubles.

MUMBO. mumbo-jumbo *useless 'tamasha'; any objects of foolish worship*

- Ritualism in religion is mumbo jumbo.
- Sanjeev Gupta preferred to marry without the usual mumbo-jumbo.

MURDER. murder will out *murder cannot be hidden for long, truth will come to light*

- You can kill a man but you cannot get rid of the guilt, because sooner or later, murder will out.

to murder truth *to destroy truth*

- Many columnists are paid to murder truth but they seldom succeed for long, because sooner or later, the truth prevails.

MUSCLE. **to muscle one's way into** *to gain entrance by physical strength*

- The dacoit muscled his way into the banquet hall.
- Many undesirable people muscle their way into power.

muscle power *physical strength*

- Nobody can vanquish the world through sheer muscle power.
- Muscle power is very much in evidence in the elections.

MUSIC. **to face the music** *to accept the unpleasant consequences at their worst; to brave a trying situation or hostile reception*

- If you have annoyed your boss, you should be ready to face the music of his indignation.

MUST. **to be a must** *to be compulsory; to be very important*

- It is a must to be a graduate before one can sit for the IAS competitive examination.
- For the young crowd, an evening at the discotheque is a must.

MUZZLE. **to muzzle the truth** *to stop the truth from spreading*

- Bureaucrats are trained in various methods of muzzling the truth.
- The usurper muzzled the truth by taking control of the radio station.

MYRIADS. **myriads of** *vast number; countless*

- There are myriads of stars in the heaven.

MYTH. **to be a myth** *false*

- The news about a ghost in the house appears to be a myth.

- The Government's claim of holding the price line has proved to be a myth.

N

NAIL. **to strike the nail on the head** *to touch the exact point*

- By giving me the exact name, you have struck the nail on the head.

drive a nail in one's coffin *to do something to hasten one's death or ruin*

- The revolutionary leader drove a nail in the coffin of autocracy by proclaiming a sovereign people's republic.

NAMBY. **namby-pamby** *feebly, wishy-washy, sentimentally childish; sentimental writing or talk*

- There was no sincerity about the condolence meeting. It was all namby-pamby.

NAME. **to be without name** *to be unknown*

- Millions die without a name.

name writ in water *one easily forgotten*

- Keats left this epitaph for himself: "Here lies one whose name is writ in water."

to die nameless *to die without reputation; to pass away in dishonour*

- Most great dictators have died nameless.

NAP. **to steal a nap** *to manage to sleep a little*

- Napoleon could steal a nap on horseback.
- People often steal a nap while commuting.

NARROW. **narrow escape** *a slight or close escape from being arrested, death, etc.*

- The police surrounded the house of the dacoit but he managed to have a narrow escape.
- The pedestrian had a narrow escape from death on the road.

to watch narrowly *to keep a close guard; to watch vigilantly*

- The constable watched the prisoners narrowly.

NAUGHT. to come to naught *to fail; to end in smoke*

- The doctor's efforts to save the patient came to naught.

to set at naught *to give no importance to; to degrade; to waste; to result in nothing, to neutralise*

- He set at naught the great opportunities that his family provided for him.

NAUSEA. to cause nausea *to inspire disgust*

- Much that is happening in the country today is enough to cause nausea.

NEAT. neat and clean *perfectly clear, nice and well-ordered*

- Your examination answer books should be neat and clean to secure good marks.

NECESSARY. a necessary evil *something which is not advisable but has to be done nevertheless*

- Marriage is a necessary evil.

NECESSITY. to make a virtue out of necessity *to do willingly what cannot be avoided*

- When an armed dacoit enters the house, make a virtue out of necessity and offer him the warmest hospitality, and the trick may work.

NECK. neck or nothing *to stake everything on an object*

- It was neck or nothing for the Mizo leader.

to take by the neck *to capture tightly*

- When you get a good job, you can take life's problems by the neck.

NECTAR. to be the nectar of *to be the sweet juice of*

- You will find peace and joy as the nectar of the hard struggle for existence.

NEED. it need hardly be mentioned *there is no need to say*

- It need hardly be mentioned that a man without money leads a miserable existence in the modern world.

NEEDLE. to needle through *to live carefully and encourage unity rather than friction among friends*

- It is best to needle your way through life instead of carving a career and treading on other people's toes.

the prick of a needle (or a pin) *a source of irritation*

- The crying of a child was the prick of a needle to her.

NEEDY. needy and greedy *poor and avaricious*

- Most *fakirs* of today are needy and greedy.

NEGOTIATE. to negotiate a corner *to go round a corner*

- A speeding vehicle should negotiate a corner carefully.

NEIGHBOUR. to neighbour on *to be close to*

- Poverty and crime neighbour on each other.

NEITHER. neither nor *neither one thing nor another, to be without both*

- I have neither a pen nor a pencil.

NERVE. to keep one's nerve *to remain calm and controlled*

- It is a test of your character to keep your nerve, whatever might happen to you or to your near and dear ones.

to lose one's nerve *to lose composure or balance*

- When one loses one's nerve, one finds the world going dark.

a matter of nerve *a fact of self-confidence*

- It is a matter of nerve to walk upon a narrow wall.

NET. to catch in the net *to trap*

- At last, the police caught the criminal in the net.

to net a profit *to make profits*

- The hoarders are netting huge profits.

NEVER. ne'er-do-well (never do well) *a good-for-nothing*

- Most youngsters of today are ne'er-do-wells.

NIBBLE. to nibble at something *to eat or destroy something slowly*

- The girl nibbled at the bread.
- Rust nibbled away at the iron door.

NICK. in the nick of time *at the last moment*

- I reached the station in the nick of time.
- They got the patient to the hospital in the nick of time.

NIL. to come to nil (or to nought) *to come to nothing; to be useless*

- All my efforts to educate the boys came to nil.

NIMINY. niminy-piminy *affectedly fine or delicate, mincing*

- She is a niminy-piminy young maiden.

NINCOMPOOP. nincompoop *a feeble foolish person*

- There is no place in modern society for a nincompoop.

NINE. a nine days' wonder *something that astonishes everybody for the moment, a short-lived spectacle*

- A victory in war is often a nine days' wonder.

a cat with nine lives *something long-lasting or enduring*

- An ousted political figure is often a cat with nine lives.

NIP. to nip in the bud *to destroy at the start*

- Evil should be nipped in the bud.

nip and tuck *neck and neck; full speed*

- It is a nip and tuck race between the 'haves' and the 'have-nots'.

NITWIT. nitwit *a fool, an idiot, a blockhead*

- Many nitwits are occupying high ministerial posts

NO. to say no *to deny; to refuse a favour*

- Miserable is the man who dare not say no to anybody.

NODDY. noddy somebody *a big foolish man*

- There is many a noddy somebody in the Public Works Department.

NOISE. to make a noise about *to propagate*

- He is making much noise about his new discoveries in science and religion.

NONE. none the worse for *not suffering, not at a disadvantage*

- They are none the worse for having lost the hockey match, because they won in tennis.
- The children are none the worse for being drenched in the rain.

NONSENSE. to make nonsense of *to prove the absurdity of*

- Political dishonesty makes nonsense of the concept of serving the people in public offices of trust.

NOSE. to lead by the nose *to govern in perfect obedience*

- No ruler can lead the modern people by the nose.

to nose around *to smell secrets; to spy*

- Why are you nosing around the conference hall?

NOT. not to speak of *not mentioning at the moment*

- Not to speak of ten rupees, I do not have even a rupee in my pocket at the moment.

NOTCH. top-notch *great; high; topping*

- He is a top-notch officer in the Government of India.

NOTHING. to come to nothing *to bear no results*

- All my efforts to promote his career have come to nothing.

NOTWITHSTANDING. notwithstanding *in spite of*

- He could not get promotion, notwithstanding his influence with the high-ups.

NOURISH. **to nourish ill-will** *to harbour a grudge*

- Defeated leaders nourish much ill-will against the victors.

NOW. **now or never** *done immediately or forgotten forever*

- When you beg a favour from anyone, it is my experience that it is now or never.

NUDE. **in the nude** *naked*

- The hippies danced in the nude on the Mall in Shimla.

NULL. **null and void** *of no legal force; ineffective; annulled*

- The old British regulations have now become null and void.

NURSE. **to nurse a grievance** *to ponder over or remember a complaint*

- Don't nurse a grievance against your parents and children for whatever reason.

NUTSHELL. **in a nutshell** *in brief*

- This book covers the whole subject in a nutshell.
- Let us put the whole matter in a nutshell for the publicity hand-out.

O

OAK. **man of oak** *a man of stern but sterling character*

- George Washington was a man of oak.

OARS. **to put in one's oars** *to interfere in another's business*

- When the boss is at work, don't put in your oars.

to rest on one's oars *to stop working temporarily*

- You cannot rest on your oars till you have reached the shore.

OASIS. **an oasis in the desert** *something of hope and promise in an otherwise fruitless and hopeless place*

- Gandhi was an oasis in the desert for India.
- Her promise of help was like an oasis in the desert.

OATH. **to take an oath** *to utter or bind oneself by an oath*

- He took an oath to stand by me in any eventuality.
- He took an oath never to drink after his father's death.

upon oath *under the obligation of an oath*

- He revealed the secret upon oath.

OATS. **to sow one's wild oats** *to commit youthful excesses or follies*

- After sowing his wild oats, a youth generally acquires prudence.

OBEDIENCE. **in obedience to** *obeying*

- The soldiers laid down their arms in obedience to the command of the general.

OBEISANCE. **to do, make, or pay obeisance to** *give salutation, bow or courtesy*

- The students should pay obeisance to their teachers.
- Make an obeisance to the deity.

OBEY. **to obey an impulse** *to be actuated by instinct*

- Those who obey an impulse often work at lightning speed.

OBJECT. **to object to** *protest*

- You should not object to what a person spends if he has earned it himself.

object of (somebody's) scorn *butt of laughter*

- If you make somebody an object of scorn, one day he will also do the same to you.

OBLIGATION. **under obligation to** *indebted to, grateful, etc.*

- I am under a great obligation to you for your help in my difficulty.

OBLIQUITY. **moral obliquity** *deviation from moral rectitude*

- The youth of today often suffer from moral obliquity.

OBLIVION. **to cast into oblivion** *to forget*

- When you rise in life, do not cast your old friends into oblivion.

OBLIVIOUS. to be oblivious of *to be oblivious of or to be forgetful*

- Good boys are never oblivious of their duties to their parents.
- He was concentrating on his work, oblivious to the noise around him.

OBSCURE. obscure Milton *one who is a genius unrecognised by the people*

- Obscure Miltons are quite often born on the college campus.

OBSCURITY. in the clouds of obscurity *unknown to the people*

- For many long years George Bernard Shaw was hidden in the clouds of obscurity.

OCCASION. to take occasion *to take advantage of an opportunity*

- When an American reporter met her, the minister took occasion to defend India's stand on the Arab problem.

to give occasion to *to give rise to*

- When a guest is in the house, do not give occasion to a domestic difference.

on occasion *in case of need, as occasion offers*

- They held receptions on occasion.

OCCULTATION. to suffer occultation *to disappear from view or notice*

- Every minister suffers occultation when he retires.

OCCUPATION. in occupation of *in possession of*

- It is not easy to dislodge somebody who is in legitimate occupation of a flat.

to be occupied with *to be busy with*

- I am fully occupied with the writing of this book.

OCEAN. **to put an ocean into a nutshell** *to express a big idea or subject briefly*

- The *Bhagavad Gita* puts an ocean into a nutshell.

to cross the oceans *to undertake a very difficult task*

- A youth in love will cross the oceans for the sake of his beloved.

OCTOPUS. **to be an octopus** *to have vast controlling power like the sea animal with eight long arms around his mouth*

- Big industrial monopoly houses are like octopuses in global power politics.

ODD. **odds and ends** *small things; small jobs*

- When a worker returns from work, he also needs to attend to many odds and ends in the home.

any odd one *any single one, one only*

- Have you some bread? I need any odd one.

ODOUR. **in bad odour** *in bad reputation*

- The dismissed servants are in bad odour.

OEDIPUS. **Oedipus complex** *excessive love for the mother, in competition with the husband, a psychoanalyst's term for the son's desire for the mother*

- Almost every grown-up son comes into conflict with the father because of the Oedipus complex.

OF. **of late** *recently*

- He has come to our neighbourhood of late.

of one mind *unanimous*

- They are of one mind about punishing the erring partner.

OFF. **off and on** *now and then*

- He comes to my house off and on.
- She visits us off and on.

to take a day off *to get away from work for a day*

- They took a day off to celebrate the marriage.

to be off *to be about to go away*

- I am off to the office in a minute.

Off with you. *Be off! Go away.*

- You cannot say to your son, "Off with you!"

OFFENCE. to take offence *to mind*

- Please mind your language and don't take offence.

without offence *without causing affront*

- Even criticise your enemies without offence.

OFFHAND. offhand *without preparation*

- The ministers deliver their speeches offhand.
- I cannot give you an exact estimate offhand.

OFFING. in the offing *near; about to take place*

- Great changes are in the offing.
- A change of job is in the offing for him.

OFFSHORE. offshore *at some distance from the shore*

- We landed offshore at Bombay on January 9th.

OIL. to pour oil on (or over) troubled waters *to pacify, to restore peace; to remove the cause of quarrel*

- When something goes wrong in the family, it is best to pour oil on troubled waters.

to add oil to the flame (similar to adding fuel to the fire) *to aggravate fury, passion, etc.*

- Even when enemies are quarrelling, don't add oil to the flame.

to burn the midnight oil *to study or work till late into the night*

- Students burn the midnight oil when the examination draws near.

to oil the wheels *to increase the pace of progress*

• Bureaucratic bribery oils the wheels of business.

to oil the fist *to bribe (same as 'to grease the palm')*

• You cannot get something done for yourself without oiling somebody's fist.

to oil one's tongue *to use flattering speech*

• You have to oil your tongue to please the boss.

OLD. Old Year's day *the last day of the year that is ending*

• Let's go up the hill and meditate on Old Year's day.

Old World *Asia and Europe (also spelled olde worlde)*

• Civilisation has spread from the Old World to the New World (America).

old is gold *old things and values are dear to us*

• This refrigerator is very old but is in a very good condition — old is gold.

old bird *a person who has become knowing through experience*

• An old bird is not easily caught in a young net.

old maid *an elderly spinster*

• If a woman does not marry, she grows up to be an old maid.

old-fangled *old-fashioned, generally 'ideas'*

• This is old-fangled furniture.

• Old-fangled ideas cannot last in the modern world.

to be an old woman *a man of timid and fussy character*

• Beware of this man. He is an old woman.

OLDEN. Olden is golden. *old age has wisdom and experience; tried and true*

• Olden is golden. — Your grandfather did give me very sound advice!

• Old friends are olden and golden.

OLIVE. olive branch *an emblem of peace*

- The general of the defeated army waved the olive branch to signify truce.

OMEGA. **from alpha to omega** *from A to Z; everything*

- I have read English literature from alpha to omega.

OMNIBUS **omnibus edition** *a book that contains everything on a subject or everything written by an author.*

- This is an omnibus edition of Hardy's works.

OMNIUM. **omnium-gatherum** *(colloquial Latin) where everybody is present*

- A marriage is a family omnium-gatherum.

ON. **on all fours** *on hands and feet, like an animal*

- The child walks on all fours.
- The father went down on all fours to play with his toddler.

on the cards *expected*

- It is on the cards that this young scholar will go to Oxford for higher studies.
- A State visit by the President is on the cards.

on the cheap *humiliating; cheap, cheaply*

- It is on the cheap to beg for money from your rivals.

on the instant *instantly*

- When I asked him for money, he gave me some on the instant.

on the move *marching, making progress*

- India is on the move.
- The army is constantly on the move in the Eastern Sector to defend our frontiers.

on the whole *taken altogether or roundly*

- India is not a backward country on the whole.

on an average *approximately*

- Everybody here earns Rs. 599 on an average.

on and off *putting on and taking off, intermittent action*

- The electric current in Delhi is on and off very often.
- This boy is on and off his job.

ONCE. once upon a time *in very olden days (standard opening for fairy stories)*

- Once upon a time, India was known as the land of milk and honey.

OPEN. an open book *keeping nothing secret*

- The life of Mahatma Gandhi was an open book.

with open arms *with great love and/or affection*

- They received us with open arms.
- The relieving force was welcomed with open arms.

in the open court *in the public court of justice*

- The desperadoes are facing trial in the open court.

with open eyes *in full awareness*

- He saw everything with open eyes.
- He entered into the conflict with open eyes.

open letter *a letter addressed to an individual but published in a newspaper usually as a matter of public interest*

- *Blitz* publishes open letters to ministers every week.

with open mouth or open-mouthed *gaping with wonder*

- When the whole class failed in the test, they were left with open mouths.
- The spectatators watched the gliding display open-mouthed.

to open up the ground *to break up surface of land by ploughing; to prepare for*

- The liberal Government has opened up the ground for globalisation.
- Tractors have opened up the ground for agriculture.

open door *freedom of admission*

- The house of God must have an open door even for the untouchables.

to open one's heart *to express one's feelings*

- Everyone of us opens his heart to a sincere friend.

OPINION. a matter of opinion *a disputable point*

- The success of a political party is a matter of opinion.

OVER. over and above *besides*

- He gets a dearness allowance over and above his salary.

P

PACE. to keep pace with *to march side by side with*

- We must keep pace with the latest scientific developments.

to put someone through her/his paces *to let her/him show what she/he can do*

- The young bride is being put through her paces to see how she can help her in-laws.

PAIN. to take (great) pains *to do with great earnestness*

- They took infinite pains for his reception.

on pain of death *on the punishment of death*

- He had to commit a murder on pain of death.

to put out of pain *to kill a suffering person or animal*

- She prayed to the doctors to put her out of pain.

PAINT. to paint black *to represent as evil or wicked*

- Even the truth can be painted black by propaganda.

PAIR. to show a clean pair of heels *to run away*

- When the principal came, the students showed a clean pair of heels.

PALM. to bear away the palm *to win victory*

- The Red Chicks bore away the palm in the cricket match.

to yield the palm *to accept defeat*

- The old-timers yielded the palm to the young Pandorans in a week-end cricket match at Bombay.

to palm off *to pass off by way of trickery*

- A ten-rupee note was palmed off as a hundred-rupee note by a rogue last night at the Wayside Hotel.
- She palmed off the clothes she didn't want on to me.

PALSIED. palsied old age *old age suffering from paralysis*

- Youth must be ready for palsied old age forty years hence.

PAMPER. to pamper to one's tastes *to over-indulge; to give in to somebody's preferences*

- It is not good to pamper to children's whims in everything.

PANDORA. Pandora's box *a box containing all ills of human life*

- Modern sophisticated technology is a Pandora's box.

PANIC. to cause panic *to create fear*

- The floods caused panic among the residents of the floodhit areas.

PANT. to pant after *to gasp with desire*

- The young man is panting after wealth and wine.

PANTS. with one's pants down *naked; humiliated*

- The smuggler was caught with his pants down.

PAPER. to commit to paper *to write down*

- This agreement should be committed to paper.

to put pen to paper *to commence writing; to write*

- While I dictate, please put pen to paper.

on paper *in writing*

- The whole discussion should be on paper.

to send (or put) in one's papers *to resign*

- When he lost the club elections, he sent in his papers.

PARADE. to make a parade of *to display ostentatiously*

- They made a parade of the huge dowry they received.

PARAGON. a paragon of virtues *a model of perfection or supreme excellence*

- Man is not a paragon of virtues.
- Indian men look for a paragon of virtues in their brides.

PARE. to pare to the quick *to cut the skin so deep as to hurt*

- Her sharp remark pared me to the quick.

to pare and burn *to cut grass and burn it for manure*

- The meadow was pared and burnt.

PARI PASSU. pari passu *side by side, at an equal rate of progress; with equal pace*

- It is truly ironical that when education and culture go up, the rate of crime goes up *pari passu* in society.

PARLEY. to parley with *to negotiate for peace; speak with another; to treat or confer with an enemy or opponent*

- After the battles are lost or won, the rival armies must parley with each other for permanent peace.

PARSNIPS. fine words butter no parsnips *no good result can come out of mere talking favourably*

- The officer was very kind and talked favourably, but fine words butter no parsnips.

PART. to have a part in *to share in; to partake of*

- All of us have a part in the social corruption seen in every sphere of life today.

to play his part *to act as or like*

- In any marriage ceremony, a priest must play his part.

to act or play a part *to perform a function; to pursue a course of action*

- In a marriage ceremony, the bridegroom must act the part of a hero returning home with the booty.

for my part *as regards my share in the matter; as far as I am concerned*

- For my part, I will cooperate fully with you for the fulfilment of your great responsibility.

in part *partly*

- I can make you the payment in part today. You can take the balance tomorrow.

on the part of *on the side of*

- It is not good on the part of one businessman to rob another.

PARTAKE. to partake of *to participate in*

- You should partake of dinner with us before you leave for your tour around the world.

PARTING. parting of the ways *separation; a point at which a fateful decision must be made*

- In August 1947, India and Pakistan stood at the parting of the ways.

parting-point *place of separation*

- A bitter quarrel is the parting-point between friends.

PARTNERSHIP. in partnership with *in the company of; enjoying a share*

- The politician committed this crime in partnership with a gang of criminals.

PARTY. to be a party to *to share the responsibility of*

- A father is usually not a party to the evil-doings of his children.

PASS. to pass for *to pretend to be; to look like*

- A criminal quite often passes for a police officer.

to come to pass *to happen*

- It so came to pass that the two friends met at the station, after a lapse of over ten years.

to bring to pass *to cause to happen*

- Sincere workers can bring great things to pass.

to make a pass *to aim a short blow at, especially ineffectually; to make an unwelcome amorous advance to*

- The soldier made a pass at the knight-at-arms.
- Rajiv dared to make a pass at the young lady who was accompanying his friend.

to pass current *to be accepted by the public*

- Dollars pass current everywhere in the world.

to pass by *to go alongside of; to overlook; to ignore*

- While going home, you will pass by a tower on your right.
- The boss passed Shanker by while making a promotion.

to pass into the hands of *to be transferred*

- The father's property passes into the hands of his children after his death.

to pass the buck (slang) *to shift responsibility to someone else*

- When the director asked who would edit the new manuscript, every editor tried to pass the buck to someone else.

to pass unnoticed *to go without being seen by anyone*

- The former rulers now pass unnoticed at social gatherings.

to pass one's eye over *to glance rapidly*

- She passed her eyes over the dolls and chose the one she liked best.

to pass a wet sponge over *to obliterate the memory of*

- Let us pass a wet sponge over all that has happened hitherto and start afresh.

PASSION. to have a passion for *to have a great devotion to or love for*

- I have a great passion for poetry and flowers.

PASTURES. for greener pastures *for newer adventures; for better opportunities*

- The youth are going abroad for greener pastures.

PAT. to pat someone on the back *to give encouragement*

- The father patted the son on the back for standing first in the examination.

pat-a-cake *the words of a nursery rhyme*

- The dismissed ministers do not sit at home and sing pat-a-cake.They sharpen their weapons for the next bout.

PATCH. to patch up *to make up*

- Let us patch up our differences and begin to work together in a spirit of fraternity.

PATIENCE. to have no patience with *to be unable to bear patiently or to endure or tolerate*

- Some old people have little patience with the pranks of youngsters.

out of patience *provoked so as to have no patience any longer*

- She was out of patience with her children who badgered her for more and more money.

PATTER. to patter flash *to speak slang, to talk the jargon of thieves*

- The Americans prefer to patter flash rather than speak even standard American.

PATTERN. to pattern upon *to fashion; to model*

- Indian democracy is patterned upon the British system.

PAUSE. to give pause to *to stop, to hesitate*

- Don't give pause to your activities.

- She kept talking without giving pause for a moment.

PAVEMENT. on the pavement *be without lodging*

- Millions in Bombay are on the pavement nowadays.

PAWN. to pawn one's future *to do something which adversely affects one's future*

- Foreign loans pawn the future of a country because the service charges grow heavier and heavier with time.

PAY. to pay one back in one's own coin *to give tit-for-tat; to take vengeance upon*

- If you unjustifiably harm someone, be ready to be paid back in your own coin.

to pay for *to make up for*

- A thousand rupees will pay for your losses.

to pay off *to pay in full and discharge; to take revenge upon*

- The servants were paid off.
- The artist paid off his rival for interfering in his private affairs.

to pay out *to disburse; to punish deservedly*

- Govind paid out to his partner and took over the whole business himself.
- The teacher paid out the most mischievous boy in class.

PEACE. to make peace with *to come to terms with*

- Everybody has first to make his peace with his conscience before making peace with the world.

kiss of peace *a kiss of greeting between members of the early church; a kiss given as a sign of friendliness*

- The general sealed the truce with a kiss of peace.
- Islamic leaders frequently greet each other with the kiss of peace.

to keep the peace *to remain peaceful, not to fight*

- Police make the criminals keep the peace.

to violate the peace *to cause disorder, to break the truce, start violence*

- The police must arrest those who violate the peace.

PEAK. to peak the oars *to raise the oar-blades out of water to a vertical position*

- They peaked their oars to salute each other.

PEARLS. to cast pearls before swine *to offer a good thing to one who is incapable of appreciating it*

- "Do not cast your pearls before swine," said Jesus Christ.
- To give technical knowledge to criminals is like casting pearls before swine.

PECUNIARY. pecuniary advantages *monetary benefits*

- Politicians derive pecuniary advantages from public.

PEDESTAL. to put somebody on a pedestal *to venerate; to worship; to honour highly*

- Everywhere moneyed men are put on a pedestal

PEEP. peep of day *first appearance of daylight*

- I will pay you a visit at the peep of day.

PEG. a round peg in a square hole *a man placed in a position unsuitable or uncongenial to him*

- A technician in an administrative office is a round peg in a square hole.

a peg to hang on *a pretext for discussion*

- The subject of an essay is merely a peg to hang on.

to move/start/stir a peg *to make a move*

- If we seek total change, the youth must move a peg.

to peg to *to fix to*

- You should peg your demands to your actual losses.

PEN. to pen *to write down*

- Please pen your demands.

pen-down strike *a strike in which office workers attend office but refuse to work*

- They held a pen-down strike to put forward their demands.

penmen of God or the Holy Ghost *writers of scriptures*

- The Bible was authored by the penmen of God.

PENNY. **penny wise, pound foolish** *to save on trifles but waste large amounts*

- The celebrators of gaudy marriages are pennywise and pound foolish. They collect pennies for a lifetime for a dowry and for conspicuous spending.

a penny for your thoughts *what are you thinking*

- "A penny for your thoughts," said the groom to the bride who was in a reverie.

a penny saved is a penny earned *savings are like earnings*

- Father said to the child, "A penny saved is a penny earned."

in for a penny, in for a pound *having entered a matter, one must carry it through at any cost*

- When marriage expenses mount, we are in for a penny and in for a pound.
- When one builds a house, one must be in for a penny and in for a pound.

take care of the pennies and the pounds will take care of themselves *if you make small savings, these will in time mount to big sums.*

- If the government takes care of the pennies, the pounds will take care of themselves, and there will be no inflation and no rising prices.

to turn an honest penny *to earn some money honestly*

- It is better to turn an honest penny than to get rich quickly through dishonest means.

penny-a-line *of cheap and superficial literary quality*

- Much of modern literature is penny-a-line.

PEPPER. to pepper with *to add jokes, etc., to embellish with*

- His talk was peppered with anecdotes.

pepper and salt *of mingled black and white colour*

- His hair is pepper and salt.

PER. per force of habit *by force of habit*

- We do many things in life per force of habit.

PERIL. at one's peril *taking risk deliberately*

- We travel by air at our peril these days.

PERJURE. to perjure oneself *to be false to an oath*

- The bigwigs are not afraid of perjuring themselves in court. (Bigwigs — very important people.)

PERSONA. persona grata *an acceptable person*

- A diplomat has to be persona grata in the country to which he is accredited.

persona non grata *an unacceptable person*

- A diplomat engaged in spying is persona non grata in the country of his assignment.

PERSPECTIVE. to look through the wrong end of a perspective *to look upon something as of less importance than it is*

- If you consider education of no material importance to you, you are looking through the wrong end of a perspective.

PETTICOAT. in petticoat *symbol of female character*

- Soldiers cannot dress up in petticoats.

petticoat government *when the ladies exert much influence behind the scenes*

- When he threw off the petticoat government of his early years, Akbar became a great ruler.

PHALANX. in a phalanx (The phalanx was a formation in which

Greek and Roman soldiers fought.) *a set of persons united together for a common purpose*

- Criminals as well as politicians work in a phalanx.

PHILOSOPHER. philosopher's stone *something which turns base metals into gold*

- There is no better philosopher's stone than the *Bhagavad Gita* for a human being.

PICK. pick of the basket *a very chosen thing or substance*

- This mango is the pick of the basket.
- Being the eldest, he always expected to be given the pick of the basket.

to pick a hole in something *to criticise, find fault with*

- It is not good to pick a hole in somebody's work.

pick-me-up *a stimulating alcoholic drink*

- They served a pick-me-up to the guests.
- The nurse said, "You need a good pick-me-up."

PICKLE. in pickle *in preparation for use*

- When a device fails, we should have something in pickle.

PIECE. to take to pieces *to separate into parts*

- The mechanic took the clock to pieces.

piece of flesh *a human being*

- You cannot expect much less from a piece of flesh.

by the piece *at the rate of per unit*

- Readymade garments are sold by the piece.

to come to pieces *to break up; to disintegrate*

- If political parties continue to wrangle, India will come to pieces.
- The ancient manuscript came to pieces even as they were examining it.

PIG. **to buy a pig in a poke** *to buy something without examining it or knowing its value*

- We are often persuaded by shopkeepers to buy a pig in a poke.

please the pigs *if all is well*

- Please the pigs, we shall meet next Saturday.

to carry pigs to market *to do business or attain results*

- Every technocrat tries to carry pigs to market.

to bring one's pigs to a pretty market *to sell at a loss*

- As there was no demand for pork, I chose to bring my pigs to a pretty market and stave off further losses.

pigs and whistles *fragments, trivialities*

- A student must not waste his time on pigs and whistles.

PIGEON. **to pluck a pigeon** *to fleece an unsuspecting or simple person*

- Most shopkeepers try to pluck a pigeon when they get a chance.

PIKESTAFF. **as plain as a pikestaff** *quite clear or plain*

- Your course of action now is as plain as a pikestaff.

PILE. **to make a pile** *to earn much money*

- She made a pile in the garment export industry.
- Dhirubhai Ambani really made his pile very astutely.

in a pile *in a heap*

- Papers lay in a pile in the office.

to pile on the agony *to overdo the painful effects by accumulation; to add fresh elements to an already painful situation*

- Poverty piles on the agony of a mother.

PILL. **pill and poll** *to ruin by extortions; to rifle; to pillage*

- Policemen usually pill and poll shopkeepers, taxi-drivers, scooter-cycle-rickshaw drivers and hand-cart men.

a sugar-coated pill *bitter advice or anything given in a sweet, persuasive manner*

- A grandmother's advice to a spoilt child is usually a sugar-coated pill.

PILLAR. from pillar to post *from one state of difficulty to another; hither and thither*

- The unemployed are driven from pillar to post.

PILLOW. pillow-fight *the sport of thumping one another with pillows*

- All the children in boarding schools greatly enjoy the pillow-fights at night.

PIN. pin-prick *act or remark intended to annoy*

- Small pin-pricks between husband and wife frequently lead them to the divorce court.

PINE. to pine for *to long for*

- The child pines for his mother.
- We often pine for things which are unattainable.

to pine away *to languish; to waste away, to die a lingering death*

- Many patriots pine away in jails.

PINK. in the pink *in perfect health or condition*

- Our children are in the pink despite this unprecedented cold wave.

in the pink of health *very healthy; having a healthy rosy colour*

- They returned from their foreign trip in the pink of health.

PINNACLE. pinnacle of power *height of power*

- Stalin gradually reached the pinnacle of power and stayed there until his death.

PIPING. piping hot *very hot, hissing hot, usually hyperbolically*

- C.R. was fond of piping hot coffee.
- In winter meals should be served piping hot.

PITH. pith of the problem *chief part*

- Crime, unemployment and rising prices are the pith of the problems that faces our leaders.

PITTED. to be pitted against *to face a challenge*

- The rival candidates were pitted against each other in the last elections.

PLAY. to play second fiddle *to be of secondary importance to; to play a subordinate part in anything*

- A secretary in the government plays second fiddle to a minister.

to play ducks and drakes with *to waste, to squander; to spend extravagantly*

- Do not play ducks and drakes with your parents' money.

PLOD. to plod along *to walk, study or work doggedly, steadily and laboriously*

- Everybody plods along in life to fulfil his destiny.

PLOUGHSHARES. to turn swords into ploughshares *to end war and replace it by peace between the warring factions*

- India and Pakistan have not yet succeeded in turning their swords into ploughshares.

PLUCK. An ounce of pluck is worth a ton of luck *It is better to have a little courage and initiative to do things rather than depend upon destiny to make you rich.*

- They do well in life who depend upon effort and not luck, because an ounce of pluck is worth a ton of luck.

to pluck a bird *to remove the feathers of a bird*

- A fowl has to be plucked before cooking.

to get plucked *to lose; to fail; to be defeated*

- The boy got plucked in the examination.

PLUS. plus fours *baggy knickerbockers; a style of men's clothes*

- Gandhiji said to the people of London: "You wear plus fours, I wear minus fours."

plus and minus *assets and liabilities*

- What were the pluses and minuses of his stint as manager of the steel plant?

PLY. to ply a trade *to follow a profession*

- Byron wrote:
- "Ply some other trade
- Save censure, for critics are all readymade."
- People are ashamed to ply their trade.

POCKET. to pocket an insult or affront *to submit to an insult without retaliation or showing displeasure*

- There are occasions when the bravest have to pocket an insult without protest.

in one's pocket *within one's control*

- The son had his doting mother in his pocket.

in pocket (opp: **out of pocket)** *with money*

- I am in pocket today.

POINT. to the point *exactly; precisely*

- Mahatma Gandhi always talked to the point.

point for point *exact in all particulars*

- The plans of attack drawn up by the contending generals were found to be point for point.

to point out *to show*

- The detective pointed out the thief to the police.

to carry the point *to be victorious in an argument*

- The lawyer carried the point in court.
- You cannot always carry the point in a debate.

upon the point *upon the subject*

- They talked upon the point for hours.

to make a point *to make a convincing argument*

- Your coming late because of rain does not make a point.
- With the arrest of the Pakistani agent, the Indian Government was able to make a point.

from one's point of view *as one considers*

- From my point of view, poverty is power.

POISON. to poison one's ears *to backbite; to talk against; to prejudice*

- He poisoned the ears of the king against his enemies.
- In family squabbles people try to poison their relatives' ears against each other.

POKE. to poke one's nose in *meddle; to interfere*

- One should not poke one's nose in the affairs of others.

POLE. from pole to pole *all over the world*

- Democracy rules supreme from pole to pole.
- Certain values remain the same from pole to pole.

to be a Pole star *to serve as a guide*

- Let your guru be the Pole star in your life.

POMP. pomp and show *display; showiness*

- A marriage is celebrated with much pomp and show these days by the newly rich.

POMPOM. pompom *a quick-firing gun, a machine-gun*

- The pompom was used to frighten away the rowdy crowds in the city square.

POOHPOOH. poohpooh *to ridicule, making light of*

- He was poohpoohed by the villagers as he drove along.
- The police officer poohpoohed the threat of kidnapping.

POOL. **to pool one's resources** *to make a collective effort*

- The industrialists should pool their resources to provide employment for the under-privileged.

POPPETY. **hoppety-poppety** *foolish, a simpleton*

- A villager is no longer hoppety-poppety.

POPPYCOCK. **poppycock** *nonsense, balderdash*

- All that you have said is mere poppycock, I am afraid.

PORE. **to pore over books/maps/documents** *to read with great attention*

- Students pore over books when the examination is near.
- The archaeologists pored over the ancient manuscripts.

POST. **post-haste** *with all speed, immediate, quick*

- He went post-haste to give the news of his promotion to his mother.

post-mortem *medical examination after death, reviewing a situation after it is over*

- The police took away the dead body for a post-mortem.
- Let us conduct a post-mortem on the failure of our scheme.

POT. **pot-pourri** *a mixed stew; mixture of sweet-scented materials, chiefly dried petals; a literary or musical production composed of unconnected parts*

- Education is a pot-pourri of different disciplines.
- The orchestra played a pot-pourri of melodies.
- The pot-pourri in the porcelain jar made the room fragrant.

POTTER. **to potter about** *to busy oneself in a desultory way; to dawdle*

- The outgoing ministers pottered about their portfolios.
- My father loves to potter around in the garden.

POW-WOW. **pow-wow** *a conference, a rite, often with feasting (from North American Red Indians)*

- The generals held a pow-wow to stop the war.
- The Indians held a pow-wow in their tepee.

PRACTICE. **in practice** *in actual working*

- Dowry is still prevalent in practice.

out of practice *out of use; no longer adept*

- Barter is out of practice nowadays.
- I am out of practice in badminton.

practice makes a man perfect *one becomes perfect in some art or craft by practising it regularly*

- The princess is a very good markswoman—practice makes one perfect.

PRACTISE. **practise what you preach** *do yourself what you ask others to do*

- It is easy to advise others but difficult to practise what you preach.

PRAISE. **self-praise is no commendation** *if you praise yourself, it does not mean that you are praiseworthy*

- He said he is a very good salesman but self-praise is no commendation.

PRECIPITATE. **in a precipitate manner** *hurriedly, hastily, suddenly*

- They left the house in a precipitate manner because of the panic caused by the fear of bombing.

PRECISE. **concise and precise** *clear and exact*

- Your statements in court should be concise and precise.

PRESENT. **to make a present** *to give as a gift*

- They made a present of a crown to Julius Caesar.

PRESUMPTUOUS. **presumptuous on someone's part** *to be arrogant*

- It is presumptuous on your part to claim that you alone are capable of doing this.

PRETENCE. to make a pretence of *to make a show of*

- When the king died, everyone made a pretence of personal loss and sorrow.
- The little boy made a pretence of crying to catch his mother's attention.

PREVAIL. to prevail upon *to persuade*

- They prevailed upon the minister to resign and seek re-election in the interests of the public.

PRIG. prig sprig *conceited child*

- He was a prig sprig with a rich father.

PRIMA. prima donna *chief female singer, the leading lady in an opera*

- Anna Pavlova was a famous prima donna.

PRINT. in print *published in a book or newspaper*

- I have read your speech in print.

PROCESSION. in a procession *many men all together*

- They went to the President in a procession to demand control of prices.

PROFIT. to profit by *to get advantage of*

- Wise men profit by others' experience.

PRONE. to be prone to *to have a leaning for*

- Those who lie are also prone to theft and murder.

PROOF. The proof of the pudding is in the eating. *a theory can only be proved in actual practice*

- You will never know the problems that come with wealth unless you are wealthy because the proof of the pudding is in the eating.

PROPAGATE. to propagate against *to run down in public estimate*

- It never pays to propagate against your employer.

PROPHET. prophet of doom *one who predicts hard times in future*

- The average economist is a prophet of doom.

PROPORTION. in proportion to *according to*

- Everybody gets rewarded in proportion to his deeds in this organisation.

PROPOSAL. to make a proposal for *to offer*

- They made a proposal for the marriage of his daughter.

PROS. pros and cons *for and against; reasons for and against*

- You must consider the pros and cons of going abroad.

PROSTITUTE. to prostitute for *to put to unworthy or wicked use*

- Don't prostitute your talent for money.

PROUD. to be proud of *to feel satisfied with*

- Do not feel proud of your power and possessions because these have no lasting value.

PROVINCE. within one's province *within one's authority or sphere of influence*

- It is not within a minister's province to save a dying man from death.

PROVISION. with the provision *on the condition that*

- He was given a pension with the provision that he should retire from active service.

PROVISO. with the proviso *on condition*

- The new party assumed power with the proviso that they would restore freedom to the people.

PRY. to pry into *to make search and inquiries; to be inquisitive about*

- Man is prying into the secrets of nature.

- No one likes to have his affairs pried into.

PULL. **push and pull** *struggle and recommendation*

- You can get no employment without push and pull.

PULP. **to reduce to a pulp** *to destroy; to make into a soft structureless mass; to pulverize*

- Old books and newspapers are reduced to pulp every year for recycling.
- After his humiliating defeat in the elections, the general's ego was reduced to pulp.

PULPIT. **to speak from the pulpit** *to lecture from a preacher's raised structure*

- You cannot speak to your children from the pulpit.

PULSATE. **to pulsate with** *throb; vibrate*

- The whole universe pulsates with life.

PULSE. **to feel the pulse** *to know the feelings*

- A true statesman can feel the pulse of the people.

PUMP. **to pump into** *to make a forcible suggestion; to invest*

- It was pumped into the head of the boy that he was the son of the king.
- The industrialist has pumped a lot of money into his new factory in Bokaro.

PUNCTUATE. **to punctuate with** *to dot; to spot; to mark with point; to emphasise*

- Life is punctuated with many frustrations.

PUPPET. **to be a puppet in the hands of** *to be controlled by*

- The king was a puppet in the hands of his courtiers.

PURPLE. **in the purple** *in high public estimation; happy and successful*

- A student is in the purple when he passes the IAS examination.

to be born to the purple *to be born with the privileges of the rich (purple was the insignia of royalty and the nobility)*

- Those who are born to the purple tend to look down on ordinary folk.

PUT. **to put across** *carry out successfully; convince*

- The point was put across to him to accept the proposal on behalf of his firm.

to put down *to write; to crush*

- Please put down whatever you want to convey to the managing director.
- The king put down the rebels with an iron hand.

to put in *introduce, insert, lodge, deposit, hand in*

- The scientist put in a new idea about satellites.
- He has put in an application for a sole selling agency.

to put in black and white *to write down*

- Every legal clause in the document must be put down in black and white.

to put off *postpone*

- Do not put off till tomorrow what you can do today.

to be hard put to it *to be in trouble or distress*

- He was hard put to it to make a living in his old age.

PYRE. **to make a pyre of** *to destroy; to burn*

- He made a pyre of his inherited property.

PYRRHIC. **Pyrrhic victory** *a victory gained at too great a cost; a victory that is worse than a defeat*

- Britain won a Pyrrhic victory in World War II, because it lost much of its empire.

Q

QUALIFY. **to qualify for** *to be fit for*

- If you do not pass M.A. in first class, you will not qualify for the job of a professor in a Delhi college.

to have qualifications for *to be suitable for*

- She has all the qualifications for a suitable bride for the eligible young man.

QUARREL. to quarrel with one's tools *not to know how to use one's tools*

- A bad workman quarrels with his tools.

at quarrel *quarrelling; at loggerheads; to fall out*

- India and Pakistan are often at quarrel.
- The rival firms decided not to constantly be at quarrel with one another.

QUEST. in quest of *in search of*

- They went up the Himalayas in quest of the Yeti.
- We often turn away from urban life in our quest for peace.

QUICK. cut to the quick *offended deeply; made very angry*

- The death of a dear friend cuts us to the quick.
- When I asked him for money, he was cut to the quick.

QUILL. to drive a quill *to write*

- He earns his living by driving a quill.
- To drive a quill, one must have a flair for words.

QUIRK. a quirk of fate *trick or. twist of destiny*

- By a quirk of fate, yesterday's prisoner became the King of France.

QUIXOTE. to be a Don Quixote *to be extraordinarily romantic and adventurous for honour or fame*

- No modern man can afford to be a Don Quixote in this age of the wonders of science and technology.

R

RACE. a race against time *to do a job in as short a time as possible*

- It was a race against time to conquer Bangladesh before the arrival of U.S. 7th Fleet in the Bay of Bengal to help the Pakistani Army.
- To meet a newspaper deadline is often a race against time.

RACK. **to rack one's brains** *to think hard*

- Every housewife is racking her brains to feed the family within her budget in the face of ever-soaring prices.

RAIL. **to rail against** *to abuse, to complain about, to revile*

- It does not pay to rail against the Government. One must exercise one's judgement discreetly at election-time.

RAINY. **for a rainy day** *for hard times*

- Every man must save something for a rainy day.

RAISON D'ETRE. **raison d'etre** *the reason; the purpose of existence*

- What is the raison d'etre for getting a degree when one cannot get a job?
- Taking care of my parents is the raison d'etre of my life.

RAM. **to ram down** *to crush; to force*

- The autocratic monarch rammed down the opposition in every conceivable way.
- Mr. Barrett rammed his wishes down his children.

RANDOM. **at random** *without selection, haphazard*

- He took five apples out of the basket at random.
- The survey was conducted at random.

RANGE. **out of range** *beyond target*

- The enemy guns were out of range for the capital, Delhi.

RANT. **to rant against** *to talk noisily against; to criticise*

- Everybody is ranting against the government for the rising prices of consumer goods.

RAPTURES. **in raptures** *in ecstatic delight*

- When she won a lottery, she was in raptures.

RAT. to smell a rat *to notice something undesirable*

- When she started neglecting him, her husband smelt a rat.

RAVAGES. ravages of time *destruction caused by the passing of the years*

- Both men and mansions suffer from the ravages of time.

RAY. a ray of hope *some slender hope*

- There is a ray of hope that the shipwrecked people may still be alive somewhere.

REACH. within one's reach *attainable*

- Some employment is yet beyond the reach of any government.

REAP. to reap a reward *to get a good result or return for good deed or behaviour*

- You will always reap a reward for your honesty.

REAR. to rear one's head *to rise, to revolt*

- The rebels have reared their head.
- Recession had reared its head even in America.

REASON. for no rhyme or reason *without any valid cause*

- Many men were murdered during the revolution in Iran in 1979 for no rhyme or reason.

RECEIVE. to receive a warm welcome *to be received with affection and regard*

- Our representative received a warm welcome in Bonn.

RECEPTION. to hold a reception *throw a party to welcome someone*

- They held a reception in honour of the visiting dignitary.
- They held a reception to celebrate their son's promotion.

RECKON. to reckon upon *depend or count upon*

- If you are ever in difficulty, you may reckon on me.

to reckon with *deal with; take into account*

- Every government has to reckon with infiltrators both in times of war and in peace.

RECONCILE. to reconcile with *to be friendly after estrangement*

- Washington and Moscow are reconciled with each other.

RED. in the red *in danger; when payments exceed deposits,*

- The flood situation in Delhi is no longer in the red.
- Your account in the bank is in the red.

REFERENCE. with reference to *in regard to*

- With reference to your letter dated August 31, I cannot meet you next week.

REFLECT. to reflect (well or badly) upon *affect, cast reproach or censure upon*

- Corruption reflects badly upon the character of politicians and administrators alike.

REIGN. to reign supreme *to have full controlling power*

- Truth reigns supreme in the universe.

RENDER. to render an account *to account for*

- You should render an account of all the money taken by you from me.
- You have to render an account of all wrongdoings by the end of your life.

RESIGN. to resign from *to give up office*

- He resigned from the presidentship of the Press Club.

RESILE. to resile from *to retract from an earlier stand*

- A government cannot resile from its commitments to other countries.

RESPECT. in respect of *on account of*

- He was given a special pension in respect of his great contribution to the firm.

with respect to *having regard to*

- He was let off lightly with respect to his physical infirmity.

RESPONSE. in response to *as a reply to*

- In response to your advertisement in *The Hindustan Times,* dated March 9, I beg to apply for a situation in your esteemed office.

REST. to rest on *to depend*

- The future of India rests on the youth of the country.

RESTRAIN. to restrain from *to hold in check*

- Children should be restrained from straying and playing truant.

REVERENCE. to pay reverence to *to honour; to salute; to hold sacred*

- Sikhs pay reverence to the *Granth Sahib,* their Holy Book.
- We should pay equal reverence to all religions while following our own.

REVOLVE. to revolve around *to go round*

- The earth revolves round the sun.
- Parents' lives often revolve around their children.

RID. to get rid of *to free oneself from*

- We should get rid of mosquitoes and conquer malaria once and forever.
- It is not easy to get rid of bad habits.

RIDE. to ride over *to conquer*

- We have to ride over many problems in life.

RIFF-RAFF. riff-raff *the rabble; scum of the people; rubbish*

- It is the riff-raff that makes up the major vote banks these days.

RING. to ring in *to begin; to welcome; to usher in*

- Let us ring in the New Year.

- The change in management should ring in fresh changes in the firm.

to ring out *to usher out; say goodbye to*

- Let us ring out the old year.

to ring round *surround*

- The army ringed round the city.
- The tomb is ringed round by a grove of trees.

to ring up *to telephone*

- In case of any trouble, please ring me up at my office.

RIOT. **a riot of colour** *very colourful, of many colours*

- The garden was a riot of colour last spring.

RIP. **to rip open** *to slash or tear open; to re-open*

- The thieves ripped open the suitcase of the sleeping passenger.

RIPE. **ripe old age** *very great age*

- George Bernard Shaw died at the ripe old age of 95.

RISE. **to rise to the occasion** *to do as the occasion demands*

- Whether it is a marriage or a mourning, we have to rise to the occasion.

RISK. **at one's own risk** *at one's own responsibility*

- A surgical operation is performed at the patient's own risk.

RIVET. **to rivet one's attention** *to concentrate*

- A student should rivet his attention on his studies.
- The T.V. programme had everyone's attention riveted.

ROAST. **much boast little roast** *tall talk without adequate performance*

- To catch votes, most politicians indulge in much boast little roast.

ROB. **to rob Peter to pay Paul** *to help one man at the cost of another*

- Robin Hood and his merry men in Sherwood forest only robbed Peter to pay Paul.

ROCK. to rock the ship *to create a tumult or trouble*

- If you want to live and let live, don't rock the ship.

ROLL. to roll back *to lose hold on; to return to the original position*

- The Empire of Napoleon was rolled back in his own lifetime.
- You cannot roll back history.

ROOST. to come to roost *to recoil upon oneself*

- The misadventures of his youth have come to roost.

to rule the roost *to be supreme somewhere*

- The mother rules the roost in the house.
- Many men like to rule the roost at home.

ROOT. root and branch *completely; thoroughly*

- The Roman Empire was destroyed root and branch.

ROSES. a bed of roses *a pleasant, easy condition of life*

- For some people, life is truly a bed of roses.
- One must realise that we cannot expect life to be a bed of roses.

to gather life's roses *to seek the pleasures of life*

- Coping with the stresses of modern living does not leave us much time to gather life's roses.

to see things through rose-coloured/tinted spectacles *to see things as bright and colourful*

- Optimists always see life through rose-coloured glasses.

under the rose *in secret; in confidence*

- Many deals are concluded under the rose.

ROUGH. rough and tough *used to a hard life*

- The soldiers are rough and tough.

rough and tumble *a disorderly and violent struggle*

- Many people were injured in the rough and tumble.

a rough diamond *an uneducated/uncouth person, lacking social graces*

- A rough diamond often proves his worth later in life.

rough and ready *good enough for ordinary purposes, not too efficient*

- Sometimes even rough and ready methods yields results.

to give somebody the rough side or edge of one's tongue *to speak rudely or severely*

- His father gave him the rough side of his tongue for staying out late.
- If he doesn't behave himself, he will get the rough edge of my tongue.

to rough up somebody/something *to treat with physical violence*

- He was roughed up by hooligans.

to take the rough with the smooth *to accept both what is pleasant as well as unpleasant*

- In life, we have to learn to take the rough with the smooth.

ROUGHSHOD. **to ride roughshod over** *to treat harshly or contemptuously*

- The boss rode roughshod over the feelings of the office staff.

ROYAL. **royal road** *an easy or magnificent way*

- There is no royal road to success in life.

RUB. **to rub out** *to remove*

- Rub out the stains from the blanket.

to rub up *to freshen or brush up, to polish*

- She rubbed up her husband's coat.

to rub someone up the wrong way *to irritate or antagonise a person*

- His tactlessness rubs most people up the wrong way.

to rub salt on someone's wounds *to increase one's troubles and torments*

- If you cannot help a friend in trouble, do not at least rub salt on his wounds.

to rub shoulders *to come into social contact*

- He often rubbed shoulders with the President.
- Parents should not let their children rub shoulders with all types of people.

RUDDER. rudder of life *a steering apparatus; something to direct progress with*

- For young folk, education is the rudder of life.
- The right values form the rudder of life for most people.

RUE. to rue the day *to feel regret for not having done something; to be sorry for*

- If you do not work hard at your books now, you will rue the day when you grow up.
- I rue the day my son got mixed up with the wrong type of people.

RUIN. to go to rack and ruin *to be destroyed, reach a state of neglect and collapse*

- Many people have gone to rack and ruin for want of proper education, guidance and training.

RUMOUR. to give currency to rumour *to spread news of doubtful accuracy*

- In war-time, one can be jailed for giving currency to rumours.
- Giving currency to rumours unnecessarily can be a dangerous practice.

RUN. to run the risk of *to face the danger of*

- If a soldier runs away from the battle-field, he runs the risk of being shot dead.

RUSH. to rush through *to go through speedily*

- Students rush through their books during examination time.

RUST. to come to rust *to become idle and useless*

- Do not let your books come to rust.

RUSTLE. to rustle through *to pass through with a soft, whispering sound*

- The wind is rustling through the leaves.

RUT. in a rut *in the old unchanged process or routine*

- Most of our educational processes are in a rut.
- We should not let ourselves get into a rut either at home or at work.

out of the (or its) rut *new; radical*

- India should get out of the rut and pull the masses out of their eternal poverty.

S

SACKCLOTH. in sackcloth and ashes *in repentance; in penance*

- After having lost his kingdom, the deposed ruler went about in sackcloth and ashes for some time.
- King Henry made a pilgrimage in sackcloth and ashes after the murder of Becket.

SADDLE. in the saddle of power *in a powerful position*

- The ex-political prisoners are now in the saddle of power.

to saddle one with responsibilities *to put responsibilities on*

- The ruling party is saddled with numerous responsibilities.

SAFE. safe and sound *in full security, secure and uninjured*

- A child at home is always safe and sound.
- The unruly traffic makes it difficult for people to get home safe and sound.

SAKE. for the sake of *out of consideration for*

- Parents slog and slave for the sake of their children.

SALLY. to sally forth *to rush out suddenly; to make a sudden charge to attack besiegers*

- They sallied forth in wave upon wave on the enemy.

SALT. true to one's salt *true to one's employer*

- The servants are no longer true to their salt.
- The Gurkha soldiers are traditionally true to their salt.

with a pinch of salt *with doubt; with hesitation; to believe with some reservations*

- The judge takes what the accused says with a pinch of salt.

the salt of the earth *people with good and true values*

- People of the older generation are usually the salt of the earth.

SATISFACTION. to one's satisfaction *so that one is satisfied*

- I shall do this work to your full satisfaction.

SAVOUR. to savour of *to smack of; to have a flavour of*

- Your actions certainly savour of idealism and high-mindedness.

SAY. to say it with roses or with flowers *to say with joy and honour*

- They said welcome to him with roses.
- Saying it with flowers is a source of joy.

SCAFFOLD. to send to the scaffold *to be hanged*

- The criminal was sent to the scaffold.

SCALE. to scale down *to lower; mitigate*

- You should scale down your demands if you want your employer to accept them.

SCARECROW. scarecrow *anything set up to scare birds; a badly dressed, emaciated or grotesque-looking person*

- A poor worker is a scarecrow in elite society.
- She's looking a real scarecrow these days.

SCATTER. to scatter to the winds *to waste; to dispel; to strew; to spend extravagantly*

- He scattered all his wealth to the winds before he died.
- She has scattered the family reputation to the winds with her behaviour.

SCENT. to get the scent of *to track, to find, to get secret information*

- The police got the scent of the smugglers.

SCEPTRE. the sceptre and the crown *the rich and the ruling community (the two symbols of kingship)*

- The sceptre and crown
  Must tumble down;
  And in the dust be equal made
  With the poor, crooked scythe and spade.

SCHOOL. a school of thought *a section of philosophers; some thinkers/people*

- A school of thought believes that those who are incurably sick should be clinically killed.

SCION. scion of the nobility *a young member of a well-born family; a descendant of*

- A scion of the nobility has more opportunities in life than the riff-raff.

SCORE. on the score of *because of, by reason of*

- The boy came first in class on the score of his hard work throughout the term.

SCOT-FREE. **to go scot-free** *untaxed; entirely free from expense, injury, etc.*

- Criminals are punishable by law, but most of them go scot-free.

SCRATCH. **to start from scratch** *to begin from the very beginning*

- After his financial losses, the merchant had to start his business from scratch.

without scratch *without any injury*

- He returned from the front without a scratch.

SCREW. **to screw up your courage** *to prepare; to tighten*

- You should screw up your courage for a long struggle against the authorities to have your demands accepted.

SCRUPLES. **without any scruples** *without hesitation; without any prick of conscience*

- The bandits waylaid travellers and killed them for money without any scruples.

SCURRY. **hurry-scurry** *hot haste, confusion and bustle*

- They ran hurry-scurry to catch the train.

SEA. **to go to sea** *to become a sailor*

- He went to sea for adventure.

at sea *in a state of confusion*

- After the loss of her only child, I found her emotionally at sea.
- The children were totally at sea because the teacher had not explained the new theorem.
- I was completely at sea in the physics class.

under the sea *in deep water*

- The sailor found his grave under the sea.

SEAL. **to seal one's fate** *to decide one's fate fully and finally; to be ready for death*

- The revolutionary regime sealed the fate of many political opponents.

SEARCH. **in search of** *looking for*

- Everybody today is in search of money.

SEASON. **in season** *at the proper time*

- Mangoes are in season nowadays.

out of season *out of the proper time; not opportune*

- In the face of inflation and rising prices, a demand for increments and higher wages is out of season.

SECOND. **at second-hand** *not directly; derived from another*

- I got the news at second-hand.

second-hand *old; already used by another*

- I am fond of buying second-hand books because they are so cheap.

second to none *first*

- Subhas Chandra Bose was second to none in his love for his country.

SEE. **to see through the game** *to discover trickery*

- When somebody is cheating, it is not easy to see through the game.

SEEK. **to play hide-and-seek** *a game in which one seeks the others, who have hidden themselves; to gain and lose alternately*

- Fortune has played hide-and-seek with me.

SEE-SAW. **the see-saw of life** *alternate up-and-down motion; ups and downs*

- Babar experienced the see-saw of life before he established his kingdom in India.

SEETHE. **to seethe with trouble, discontent, etc.** *to be agitated*

- People are seething with discontent because of the rising prices.

SEIZE. **to seize an opportunity** *to make use of a chance*

- Modern man seizes every opportunity to make money.

SELF-SEEKING. **self-seeking** *seeking one's own advantage*

- There is hardly a human being nowadays who is not self-seeking.

to seek one's self *to find inner reality*

- The scriptures teach us to seek ourselves.

SENTENCE. **to sentence to death** *to order to be killed*

- The judge sentenced the murderer to death.

SET. **to set about** *to get ready to do something*

- It is time to set about your work in hand.

to set in *to start*

- Winter has set in at last.

to set up *to fix; to establish*

- They set up their camp on the hill.
- The newly elected party has set up a new government.

to set out for *to start on a journey*

- They set out for Bangkok yesterday.

to set on to *to move on; to incite; to attack; to instigate*

- They have set him on to assassinating the Shah of Iran.

to set upon *to attack*

- The dacoits set upon unwary travellers in the Pimpri forest.

to set by *to lay up; to put aside*

- Krishna set by a decent sum for the upkeep of his country house.

to set off *to go on a journey*

- They set off at noon for London.

well set *in a position*

- Mekhala is well set to join the Indian Foreign Service.

SETTLE. to settle the account *to take revenge*

- The gangsters settled the account by killing a constable.

SEVENS. at sixes and sevens *in disorder*

- When Malati returned home, she found everything at sixes and sevens; her children had gone on a rampage in her absence.

SEVERALLY. jointly and severally *collectively and individually*

- The members of a co-operative society are liable to pay back a government loan jointly and severally.

SHACKLES. in shackles *in fetters and handcuffs*

- The police put the prisoners in shackles.

SHADE. a shade of *a little of; a very minute difference*

- There is not even a shade of truth in what you say.

SHADES. shades *abode of the dead, Hades*

- The killer of millions is sure to go to the shades after his death.

SHADOW. a shadow of *a smaller version of*

- The son is a shadow of his father.

in the shadow of *under the protection of*

- The child lives happily in the shadow of his mother.

SHAPE. to take shape *to become clear; to crystallise*

- The economic policies of the government have not yet taken shape.

SHEET. to be a sheet in the wind's eye *to be intoxicated or drunk*

- Towards the fag end of his life, the poet became a sheet in the wind's eye and soon died.

SHILLING. **to cut off with a shilling** *to bequeath nothing; to disinherit*

- The miser cut off his wife with a shilling.
- The old gentleman reinstated his heir whom he had earlier cut off with a shilling.

SHIPSHAPE. **shipshape** *trim, neat, in a seamanlike condition; in good order; well arranged*

- She left the house shipshape last Sunday.

SHOESTRING. **on a shoestring budget** *with a minimum of capital; within very limited resources*

- They celebrated their marriage ceremony on a shoestring budget.
- We have been living on a shoestring budget for years.

SHOOT. **to shoot forth** *to grow*

- Plants shoot forth in spring.

to shoot down *to kill*

- They shot down the dacoits near the mouth of the ravine.

to shoot in *to interrupt*

- "When I am talking, please don't shoot in," she said to the maid.

SHORT. **to cut a long story short** *to come to the point*

- He said, "To cut a long story short, I've come to borrow some money."

SHOULDER. **to shoulder responsibilities (opp: to shrug off your responsibilities)** *to be responsible*

- The head of a family has to shoulder heavy responsibilities.

to shrug one's shoulders *to show indifference or coldness*

- When his mother made a proposal for his marriage, he simply shrugged his shoulders.

SHUT. **to shut in** *to be imprisoned*

- The two princes were shut in the Tower of London.

to shut down *to close down business*

- He had to shut down his shop because of losses.

SIDE. side by side *alongside*

- They fought side by side in the Bangladesh war.

SIGHT. at first sight *immediately*

- He fell in love with her at first sight.

at sight *as soon as seen*

- This dangerous dacoit should be shot at sight.
- They were given orders to shoot at sight.

SIGN. to sign one's own death warrant *to become responsible for one's end*

- A fat person who does not reduce his weight is signing his own death warrant.

SINGSONG. singsong *monotonous; monotonous song*

- It was a singsong function at the temple.
- The teacher spoke in a singsong voice.

SINK. to sink one's differences *to become friends again*

- Let us sink our differences and begin business anew.

SIT. to sit on the hedge/fence *to be neutral; not to take either side*

- You cannot sit on the hedge when injustice is being perpetrated.

SKELETON. a skeleton in the cupboard *an ugly thing to hide; a hidden domestic sorrow or shame*

- Every politician has a skeleton in the cupboard.

SKY-HIGH. sky-high *very high*

- Prices are soaring sky-high.

SLIP. to slip through *to escape*

- The thieves have slipped through the net.

a slip of the tongue *a mistake in speaking*

- A slip of the tongue causes laughter in a gathering.
- "A slip of the tongue is not one of the mind, And those who laugh are rude and unkind."

a slip of the pen *a mistake in writing*

- A slip of the pen in a legal document can prove costly.

SMOKE. to end in smoke *to be wasted; to come to nothing*

- All my efforts to reform Vikram have ended in smoke.

SNAKE. a snake in the grass *a hidden enemy*

- Be careful of a snake in the grass.
- Her betrayal showed her to be a real snake in the grass.

a snake (or viper) up one's sleeve *a hidden enemy closer to one than one thinks*

- Friendship with anti-social elements is a snake up one's sleeve.
- My partner turned out to be a snake up my sleeve.

SORE. a running sore *a cause of continued trouble*

- Kashmir is a running sore for both India and Pakistan.

SPEAK. to speak volumes *to be highly significant*

- Your devotion to duty speaks volumes for your religious bent of mind.

SPINE. to the spine (or core) *to the backbone; firmly*

- He is a Communist to the spine (or to the core).

SPRING. to spring a surprise *to cause astonishment; to be taken unawares*

- He sprang a surprise on us by appearing suddenly at the time of marriage.

SPRINKLE. to sprinkle salt on a wound *to intensify trouble or discomfiture*

- To demand instant payment from one who has lost her child is to sprinkle salt on a wound.

SPUR. on the spur of the moment. *suddenly; on an impulse*

- He left home on the spur of the moment.

SPY. to spy upon *to seek secret information*

- The king's men spy upon all newcomers to the country.
- Business houses often spy on each other's research departments.

SQUARE. to square up *to face upto and to tackle; to settle*

- I have squared up my account with the canteen.

to square with *tally; to put in a proper position or relation*

- You must square expenses with income.
- Russia has squared with America.

STAKE. to stake one's all *to take the maximum risk possible*

- He staked his all on going abroad.

STEAD. in one's stead *in one's place*

- His son was present in his stead at the meeting.
- The headmaster sent one of the senior teachers in his stead to attend the function.

to stand one in good stead *to serve one's needs well*

- Money stands one in good stead everywhere .

STEER. to steer clear *to keep away from*

- You should steer clear of all family entanglements.

STEM. to stem from *to come out of*

- India's troubles primarily stem from inflation.

STITCH. a stitch in time saves nine *a little remedy well in time saves a lot of trouble afterwards*

- All faults must be attended to promptly because a stitch in time saves nine.

STOCK. to take stock of *to count and assess*

- You should take stock of your time, energy and money before launching a new enterprise.

STOP. **to Stop at nothing** *to do everything; to go to any length*

- A child will stop at nothing to get his toy back.
- She will stop at nothing to get her own way.

STRAIN. **to strain one's eyes** *to see as far as possible*

- She strained her eyes in the dark to locate her purse on the table.

STRAITENED. **in straitened circumstances** *in misery; in economic hardship*

- My parents were in straitened circumstances when they put me in school.
- The father's sudden death left his family in straitened circumstances.

STRAW. **the last straw** *the final trouble*

- It is the last straw that broke the camel's back.
- When all is lost, money is your last straw to make life worth living.

a drowning man clutches at a straw *a man in trouble does anything to save himself*

- He turned to his rivals for financial help, for a drowning man clutches at a straw.

STRETCH. **at a stretch** *continuously, in one sitting*

- Once I typed for thirty-six hours at a stretch.

STRIKE. **to strike work** *to stop work to press demands*

- The workers struck work yesterday.

SUGAR. **to sugar one's words** *to flatter by talking sweetly*

- Many people achieve their objectives by sugaring their words to please the boss.

SUN. **a sunspot** *a relatively dark patch on the surface of the sun; minor defects even in the high and mighty*

- There are sunspots even in the sun; remember no one is perfect.

a place in the sun *a place of distinction; a comfortable life*

- Everyone hopes for a place in the sun.

SWADDLING. in swaddling clothes *not yet grown up; still immature*

- Many politicians still appear to be in swaddling clothes.

SWALLOW. to swallow or eat one's words *to deny what one has spoken; to omit words while reading or typing; to retract*

- Many men who voiced their support now want to eat their words to curry favour with the new bosses.
- You have swallowed many words while typing.
- He vowed that he would make his detractors eat their words.

SWEAT. by the sweat of one's brow *by honest hard labour*

- I earn my living by the sweat of my brow.

SWING. in full swing *in mid-career; in full operation*

- The community development programme is in full swing nowadays.
- Preparations are in full swing for her daughter's wedding.

SWORD. to put to the sword *to kill*

- Nadir Shah put the citizens of Delhi to the sword.
- Many mutineers were put to the sword in 1857.

T

T. to a T *fully; exactly*

- An honest man does every job of work to a T.

TABLES. to turn the tables *to bring about a complete reversal of circumstances*

- Shivaji turned the tables on the Mughal army.

TAIL. **to turn tail** *to run away*

- When trouble comes, all selfish friends turn tail.
- The coward turned tail and fled from the battlefield.

TAKE. **to take lying down** *to accept anything without protest or objection*

- Patriots never take their defeat lying down.

to take something or someone for granted *to accept without investigation; to assume*

- Do not take it for granted that I can take you with me to Washington this time.
- Children have a tendency to take their parents for granted.

to take up *to assume responsibility for; start*

- When will you take up your new assignment?

to be taken in *to be deceived*

- When the thug showed him spurious gold, he was taken in.

to take out *to diminish, to remove from within*

- Take ten out of fifteen.
- Take out her lower front tooth.

TALENT. **to have a talent for** *to have ability; special aptitude*

- I have no talent for mathematics.
- She has a special talent for looking after people.

TALK. **to talk through one's hat** *to talk wildly ar at random*

- Please stop talking through your hat.

TAR. **to tar one's name** *to cast a slur on oneself*

- Don't tar the name of your parents by doing anything silly or foolish.

TARNISH. **to tarnish the image of** *to slur one's reputation*

- Corruption tarnishes the image of any person or political party.

TARTAR. **to catch a Tartar** *to engage in a combat with a formidable, rough unmanageable person*

- When the constable attacked the gangster, he found that he had caught a tartar.

TASK. **to take to task** *to call to account; to reprove; to reprimand; to reproach*

- The accountant was taken to task for irregularities in the accounts.
- The father took his son to task over his bad school report.

TEETHING. **teething troubles** *troubles at the start of any venture*

- The nursery school is still suffering from teething troubles.

TELL-TALE. **tell-tale marks** *clues that betray or reveal*

- Every murderer invariably leaves behind some tell-tale marks.
- The tell-tale marks of a needle indicated that he was addicted to drugs.

THERE. **there and then** *immediately*

- When I asked him for some money, he gave me a thousand rupees there and then.

THROUGH. **to hustle through** *to do in a hurried, clumsy manner*

- Some car mechanics hustle through their jobs.

to go through *to read*

- Have you gone through my book?

through and through *completely, fully*

- He is a gentleman through and through.

through thick and thin *through all kinds of fortunes*

- Good friends stick together through thick and thin.

THROW. **to throw out** *to reject by votes*

- The bill was thrown out in Parliament.
- The wayward son was thrown out of the house.

TIDE. **to swim with the tide** *to follow the majority*

- During the war, most people swam with the tide.

TIDY. **to make a tidy/neat sum** *to make a lot of money*

- My grandfather made a tidy sum through agriculture.

TIE. **to tie down** *to bind down*

- A woman with small children is tied down to the house.

to tie hand and foot *to bind completely*

- The prisoner was tied hand and foot.

TIGHT. **in a tight corner** *in a difficult position*

- When Gopal's purse was picked on the train, he found himself in a tight corner.

TIP. **to tip the scales** *to increase support*

- The incredible victory of his side tipped the scales in his favour as captain.

TOLL. **to take a heavy toll** *to destroy men and property on a vast scale*

- Floods take a heavy toll every year in some parts of India.

TOM-TOM. **tom-tom or tam-tam** *an Indian drum*

- They beat a tom-tom (or tam-tam) to call the men together.
- The news was tom-tommed all over the colony. (extended use)

TONGUE. **to hold one's tongue** *to keep silent*

- If you know any secrets, it is better to hold your tongue.

TOOTH. **to fight tooth and nail** *to fight with all possible vigour and fury; bitterly*

- The women fought one another tooth and nail in the early morning brawl at the well.

TOP. **at the top of one's voice** *as loudly as one can; at full blast*

- She called out to her son at the top of her voice.

TOPSY-TURVY. **topsy-turvy** *turned upside down; confusion*

- The children made everything topsy-turvy in the house.

TRICK. **a trick of the trade** *professional secret; a knack; a trade artifice*

- Every politician uses some trick of the trade to win an election.

TRIGGER. **to trigger off a chain reaction** *one result leading to another; like atomic energy which spreads the conflagration from atom to atom*

- Anything good or bad triggers off a chain reaction in the cosmos.

TROJAN. **Trojan** *very hardworking*

- Kiron Kumar is a Trojan to his friends.
- She is capable of working like a Trojan.

TRUANT. **to play truant** *to turn away from school or office*

- Students often play truant to see a cinema-show.

TURN. **to turn in** *to go into the house; to go to bed; to enter; to bend inward*

- When do you turn in at night?

to turn off *to put out of action; to dismiss*

- Please turn off the fan after use.
- My wife turned off the undependable servant-girl.
- This kind of music completely turns me off. (extended use)

to turn down *refuse; reject*

- He turned down my offer to help him in his difficulty.

TUT-TUT. **tut-tut** *exclamation of scorn; rebuke; mild disapproval*

- When the princess refused to marry, the queen said "Tut-tut!"

U

ULCER. **to be an ulcer** *to be a corrupting influence; a moral plague-spot*

- Bribery is an ulcer in the body politic of any nation.

ULTERIOR. **ulterior motive** *beyond what is avowed or evident; on the further side*

- She has an ulterior motive in offering to help him monetarily in his difficulties.

UMBRAGE. **to take (or give) umbrage** *to offend or to feel offended*

- Don't take umbrage at what your boss says.
- When the man patted the cobra, the latter took umbrage and bit him.

UMBRELLA. **under the umbrella of** *under the patronage of*

- Many countries flourish under the umbrella of the USA.

an umbrella term *a term to indicate joint qualities*

- The Slavic Republics is an umbrella term for many small countries.

UNANIMOUS. **to be unanimous** *to be of one mind; with none dissenting*

- Men are never unanimous in offering every opportunity for self-expression to women.

UNCALLED. **uncalled for** *unprovoked; offensively gratuitous; not asked for*

- It was an uncalled for gesture on his part.

UNCANNY. **uncanny event** *an occurrence which is weird; unearthly; savouring of the supernatural*

- The appearance of a ghost is an uncanny event.

UNCLE. **to talk like a Dutch uncle** *to rebuke*

- One cannot talk like a Dutch uncle to public school students.

Uncle Sam *the United States of America or its people*

- Uncle Sam today controls half the world.

UNCLOTHE. to unclothe oneself of humanity *to become inhuman*

- Lust for power drives many to unclothe themselves of humanity.

UNDER. under the circumstances *in the existing conditions*

- A man without food and home cannot be happy under the circumstances.
- He said, "I have no choice except to resign under the circumstances."

under one's breath *in a whisper, in a low voice*

- It is best to talk under one's breath in a hospital.

under-age *below the age of majority*

- A boy is still under-age for a job at fifteen.
- You cannot claim your inheritance when you are under-age.

to go under *to be defeated; to be disgraced*

- All the challengers of Cassius Clay went under.
- Life's difficulties should not make us go under.

under arms *in the army; fighting*

- India was under arms against Great Britain.

under the table *clandestinely; dishonestly*

- Business people make many transactions under the table.

UNDERFOOT. to tread underfoot *to trample*

- Don't tread even a worm underfoot.

UNDERGROUND. to go underground *to hide; to become secret*

- During the Quit India Movement many patriots went underground to escape arrest by the British government.

UNDERSTANDING. a good understanding *amicable relations*

- India has a good understanding with the CIS (formerly USSR).

UNGAINLY. ungainly and ungodly *awkward and against God*

- Naked and wholesale materialism is both ungainly and ungodly.

UNISON. in unison with *in harmony with*

- The bureaucrats should work in unison with the ministers.

UNKINDLY. to take unkindly to *to resent; to interpret in a bad light*

- When the newspapers criticized the general, he took it unkindly.
- "I take unkindly to being treated like this," she said.

UNLESS. unless and until *not so long as*

- You cannot be happy unless and until you attain your goal in life.

UP. up the wind *towards the quarter towards which the wind blows*

- The kite went up the wind.

up hill and down dale *over hill and valley; all over an area*

- The *sadhu* went up hill and down dale in search of God, but did not search within himself.

up to *to depend on oneself to decide*

- It is up to you to come or not.

not up to much *of no ability, importance or worth*

- Without education a boy is not up to much.
- Despite his opportunities, he is not up to much in his career.

up and down *to and fro; here and there*

- The child went up and down in search of its mother.

the ups and downs *the good and bad times*

- We must face the ups and downs of our careers with equanimity.

UPPER. to keep a stiff upper lip *to show no sign of weakening*

- After losing the war, General Niazi kept a stiff upper lip.

UPSET. to upset someone's applecart *to overthrow someone's projects or plans*

- The boys upset the principal's applecart.

UPSHOT. the upshot *the final issue; outcome; result*

- The upshot of World War II was that the British lost their sprawling Empire.

UP-TO-DATE. up-to-date *extending to the present time; latest*

- This book will give you up-to-date information.

URGE. to urge through *to speed up*

- The member urged the bill through Parliament.
- The General has urged army reforms.

USE. to make use of *to employ/to avail of*

- You can make use of my pen for writing your letter.
- You can make use of my servants for the party.

to use up *to exhaust*

- All our funds have been used up.

use money *interest; service charges*

- We pay use money on foreign loans.

USHER. usher from/into *to take; to accompany*

- The lady was ushered from the room.
- The ambassador was ushered into the presence of the King.

UTILITY. public utility *a thing of public use or benefit*

- Transport services are a public utility.

UTMOST. to do one's utmost *to make one's greatest or best effort*

- He did his utmost to win a prize at the Rose show.

at the utmost *in the extremest case*

- At the utmost, you can be fined for a traffic offence.

to the utmost *to the extreme*

- Do not go to the utmost in a silly quarrel.

to the uttermost *to the maximum extent*

- The soldiers fought to their uttermost in the last war.

V

VACATION. on vacation *on holiday*

- The judge is on vacation in Kashmir.

VALUE. to set a value on *to estimate a price*

- People set a high value on prestige and power.

VANGUARD. in the vanguard *at the front*

- In every movement, the youth are in the vanguard.

VANISHING. vanishing trick *thuggery; cheating*

- The mountebank performed a vanishing trick with the people's hard-earned money.

VAPOROUS. vaporous webs *fanciful ideas*

- You cannot build the hard work-a-day world with vaporous webs.

VARIANCE. at variance with *out of harmony with, not agreeing with*

- Moneymaking is at variance with the search for God.

VARIEGATED. variegated view *a scenic panorama*

- This window offers a variegated view of the landscape.

VAULT. vault over *cover with an arched dome; to jump over*

- Heaven vaults over the earth.
- The horse and rider vaulted over the hedge and galloped out of sight.

VEHEMENCE. with vehemence *with great force*

- He spoke against the authorities with vehemence.

VEHICLE. to be a vehicle for *to be a means of communication*

- Language is a vehicle for great thoughts.

VEIL. to draw a veil over *to hide; to close a chapter*

- Let us draw a veil over the British Raj in India.

to take the veil *to become a nun*

- Frustrated or unhappy women quite often take the veil.

VELOCITY. to gain velocity *to acquire speed*

- The aeroplane gained velocity in a matter of minutes.

VENGEANCE. to wreak vengeance upon *to take revenge on*

- Men, when they come to power, cannot help wreaking vengeance on their enemies and detractors.

with a vengeance *with great force or violence*

- The soldiers fought at Thermophylae with a vengeance unknown in history.
- After his change of heart, the dacoit became religious with a vengeance.

VENT. to give vent to *to express; to pour forth; to unburden*

- Very often, students give vent to their grievances by burning buses.

VENTILATE. to ventilate one's view *to express one's ideas*

- You can ventilate your views by writing a letter to the editor of a popular newspaper.

VENTURE. at a venture *at random; by chance; without due consideration or thought*

- He luckily found a good second-hand car at a venture in Calcutta.

VERBOSITY. full of verbosity *containing superfluous words in excess of requirement*

- A minister's speech is most often full of verbosity.

VERS LIBRE. **vers libre** *free verse; verse without rhyme*

- He clothed his ideas in *vers libre.*
- *Vers libre* is often used by lesser poets.

VERSED. **well-versed in** *expert on a subject*

- She is well-versed in music.

VERTEBRATE. **vertebrate writing** *writing characterised by strength, firmness or consistency*

- Carlyle is famous for vertebrate writing.
- Investigative journalism should be backed up by vertebrate writing.

VETERAN. **veteran of war** *an experienced soldier*

- Field Marshal Manekshaw is a famous veteran of war.

VEXATION. **vexation of the mind, spirit** *mental trouble*

- A domestic difference causes a vexation of the mind.

VIA. **via media** *a middle course*

- In case of differences between friends, it is not difficult to find a via media.

VICE. **vice versa** *contrariwise, the other way round*

- Inflation leads to rising prices and vice versa.

VICISSITUDES. **vicissitudes of life** *ups and downs of life*

- Every great man passes through the vicissitudes of life.

VICTORY. **to win a victory over** *to get the better of*

- You have to win a victory over unemployment.

moral victory *a victory of truth*

- A physical defeat may actually be a moral victory.

VIE. **to vie with** *to compete with*

- Light vies with darkness in the world.
- Girls from all over the city vied with each other for the modelling assignment.

VIEW. point of view *opinion*

- What is your point of view on this subject?

in the view of *in the opinion of*

- You are a coward in the view of your friends.

on view *on exhibition; open to general inspection*

- The goods to be auctioned are on view.

to take a long view *to provide for the future*

- She is saving money for possible contingencies, taking a long view.
- Liberalisation has been introduced taking a long view of the economy.

VIGIL. to keep a vigil *to keep a watch*

- I have to keep a vigil tonight.

to be vigilant *to be watchful*

- The police must be vigilant against criminals.

VIGOUR. verve and vigour *with strength and determination*

- You should work with verve and vigour to build up your career.

VILLAINY. words of villainy *abusive language; base, unscrupulous utterance*

- Uncouth people use words of villainy.

VINCIBLE. vincible ignorance *ignorance, the means of overcoming which are possessed by the ignorant person himself*

- The Cuban elections proved that the masses suffered only from vincible ignorance.

VINDICATE. to vindicate one's honour *to justify one's honour by actual action*

- You should vindicate your honour by fulfilling the word given to your father-in-law.

in vindication of *by way of fulfilment, defence or justification*

- He went to jail in vindication of his political opinions.

vindicative of *justifying a stand*

- The judgement is vindicative of your legal stand on the case.

VIOLENCE. **to do violence to** *to injure; to harm*

- Do no violence to the scriptures.
- Frustration often leads one to do violence to somebody.

to practise violence on *to harm*

- The army must not practise violence on the civil population.

to lay violent hands upon *to harm; to hurt*

- The duke laid violent hands upon his enemies.

VIOLIN. **to play first violin** *to take a leading part*

- The crown prince played first violin in Yemen.

VIPER. **viper's brood** *a group of undesirable people*

- Gangsters are a viper's brood.

VIRGIN. **virgin's milk** *a wash for cleansing and purifying the skin*

- Virgin's milk is a chemical preparation having a milky appearance.

VIRTUE. **by virtue of** *on account of; by reason of*

- Yahya Khan had complete power by virtue of his being a dictator.

of easy virtue *of loose character*

- A prostitute is a woman of easy virtue.

to make a virtue of *to gain credit by*

- Many people make a virtue of temple-going and ritualism.

VIS-A-VIS. **vis-a-vis** *with regard to; (literally, face to face with); persons or things situated opposite each other; over against; in comparison with*

• The council discussed the war vis-a-vis the latest debacle.

VIVA VOCE. viva voce *by words of mouth; in speech; oral examination or interview*

• Many students fail in the viva voce test.

VOGUE. in vogue *customary; mode or fashion at any particular time*

• Western fashions are in vogue in most metropolitan cities of India today.

out of vogue *out of fashion*

• Knickers have gone out of vogue even among schoolchildren.

VOICE. to have a voice in *to have a say in the determination of*

• I had no voice in the marriage of my son.

the voice of God *the will or desire of God*

• The voice of the people is the voice of God.

with one voice *unanimously*

• The students voted for the picnic with one voice.

to voice one's views *to give expression to one's ideas*

• Every member of the club can voice his views.

VOLTE-FACE. volte-face *a complete change of attitude or opinion*

• Quite a few showed a volte-face after the elections.

VORACIOUS. voracious reader *one who reads everything; an insatiable or great reader*

• The voracious reader found most libraries inadequate for his purpose.

VOTE. to put to the vote *to submit to the decision of a meeting*

• The resolution was put to the vote in the general meeting and carried through.

to have a vote *to have a say in decision-making*

- The poor have no vote in running the government.

VOW. **to make a vow** *to take a pledge*

- They made a vow of living for others.

to break a vow *to violate a pledge*

- It is not worthy of an honourable person to break his vow.

VOX. **vox populi, vox Dei (Latin)** *the voice of the people is the voice of God*

- Whenever a great issue is at stake, one must rely on the adage, *vox populi, vox Dei.*

VOYAGE. **to go on a voyage** *to take a sea trip*

- My friend has gone on a voyage for health reasons

VULTURES. **to cast to the vultures** *to be dishonoured; (to be left to be eaten by birds, etc.); to be abandoned*

- An Italian dictator was cast to the vultures by the people after being murdered.
- They exploited the old woman and then cast her to the vultures.

W

WADE. **to wade through** *to walk through water, mud, etc.; to struggle through*

- The captain has waded through great hardships.

WAG. **to play the wag** *to play truant*

- Some students play the wag in schools.

how the world wags *how the affairs are going on*

- The newspapers tell us how the world wags.

to let the world wag *to regard the course of world events with unconcern*

- A *yogi* lets the world wag.
- Old people often let the world wag, having seen enough of it.

wag one's tail *to indicate approval*

- When the leader made a proposal, the henchmen wagged their tails.

WAGE. **to wage a battle** *to pledge oneself to legal combat*

- The victims of injustice waged a battle against their government

to wage a war *to launch a war*

- Pakistan waged a war against India in 1965, and again in 1971.

WAGER. **to lay a wager** *to bet*

- He laid a wager on passing the examination.

to win or lose a wager *to win or lose a bet*

- He passed the examination and won the wager.
- He lost his wager on the victory of the king's forces in a neighbouring country.

WAISTCOAT. **under one's waistcoat** *in one's breast*

- Mata Hari carried many secrets under her waistcoat.

WAIT. **to sit in wait** *to keep waiting*

- Many men sit in wait for the manager.

to lie in wait *to wait to trap*

- The police lay in wait for the dacoits.

to wait upon *to wait for personal service*

- The maidservant waited in attendance on the old woman.

to wait upon providence *to watch the turn of events*

- In politics, poor people have to wait upon providence.

WAIVE. **to waive aside/away/off** *to remove; to abolish*

- All punishments were waived off during the general amnesty.

WAKE. to wake up snakes *to cause trouble or disturbance*

- After the civil turmoil, the criminal elements are waking up snakes.

to wake out of *to become awake*

- After the death of his father, the boy was wakened out of his dreams of easy affluence.

WALE. to wale *to pick, select, choose*

- You should wale your career early in life.

WALK. a walk-over *an easy victory*

- The school eleven had a walk-over against the college eleven at the Oval.

cock of the walk *a person whose supremacy in his own circle is undisputed*

- The village schoolmaster is the cock of the walk in his village.

walk of life *a social grade, position*

- There are cheats in every walk of life.

to walk into *to enter without previous knowledge*

- The courier walked into an ambush in Burma.

to walk out with *to keep company with a view to marrying*

- She walks out with the man she loves.

to walk with God *to lead a godly life*

- Few folks walk with God nowadays.

to walk after *to direct one's conduct by, imitate*

- A child should walk after his parents.

to walk off with *to carry away as a prize,plunder,etc.; to steal*

- The man walked off with my umbrella.
- He walked off with "The Man of the Match" award.

to walk in one's sleep *to walk in a dream; to walk while dreaming*

- Those who walk in their sleep need psychiatric care.

WALL(S). to push or thrust to the wall *to force, to give place*

- The newcomers pushed the old-timers to the wall.

to go to the wall *to be hard-pressed*

- The common people have gone to the wall after the new budget.

to drive someone to the wall *to push to extremities*

- Dr. Samuel Johnson drove a ruffian to the wall.

with one's back to the wall *in desperate straits, at bay*

- The patriots fought with their backs to the wall and ultimately won a victory in spain.
- The scam found many brokers with their backs to the wall.

to turn one's face to the wall *to be on the point of death*

- My father prayed to God when he turned his face to the wall.

within the four walls *inside the house*

- The housewife is complete mistress within the four walls.
- Being in *purdah,* women often lived most of their adult lives within the four walls.

even walls have ears *there are spies everywhere*

- Be careful of what you say, because even walls have ears.

WALTZ. waltz around *to veer; to move trippingly*

- After much persuasion, he waltzed around to my point of view.

WANT. wilful waste makes woeful want *extravagance leads to poverty*

- Save while you can and save what you can, for wilful waste makes woeful want.

in no want of *having an abundance of*

- The affluent classes are in no want of good food and drink.

to want for nothing *to have no lack of necessities and comforts*

- The rich classes want for nothing.

WAR. to go to the war *to go abroad as a soldier; to go to fight in a foreign country*

- Many ex-servicemen in India have gone to the wars.

to make/wage war on *to declare war on*

- Hitler made war on Great Britain.

WARM. to keep a place warm *to occupy it temporarily or for some time until someone is ready to occupy it*

- The temporary hand kept the place warm for the clerk.

a warm reception *vigorous resistance*

- The Allied Armies received a warm reception at the hands of Rommel in the Western Desert.

WARPATH. to be on the warpath *among the Red Indians, the path followed on a military expedition; the expedition itself; to be ready to fight*

- The youth have always been on the warpath in the political field.

WASH. to wash one's dirty linen in public *not to keep a secret, to expose sordid family affairs or scandals*

- Political parties are fond of washing their dirty linen in public.
- Friends usually avoid washing their dirty linen in public.

to wash one's hands of *to disown responsibility for; to have nothing to do with (from Pilate washing his hands at the trial of Jesus Christ)*

- I have washed my hands of this sordid affair.

to wash one's brain (or brain-wash) *(slang) to drink copiously; to make one believe something different*

- Dictators wash the brains of the masses.

to wash down *to carry downward; to help swallow solid food*

- The guests washed down big plates of meat and sweets with wine at the wedding party last night.

WASTE. to make waste *to be wasteful*

- Haste makes waste.
- Careless youth makes waste of time.

to run to waste *to be wasted or lost (orig. of liquids)*

- Rivers run to waste in the seas.
- A lot of our natural resources run to waste even today.

to waste one's breath *to speak to no purpose; to produce no effect*

- When you lecture to the youth, you are only wasting your breath.

WATCH. to stand on the watch *to be watchful*

- To police must stand on the watch against drug-peddling.

to watch one's step *to step with care; to act warily*

- When young, one must watch one's step.
- In a new job, one has to watch one's step.

to watch out *to look out; be careful*

- The night sentry has to watch out for house-breakers and dacoits.

WATER. to make a hole in the water *to commit suicide by drowning*

- Many people living near seashores are tempted to make a hole in the water.

water of life *spiritual refreshment, whisky, brandy, etc.*

- Many a great man has recourse to the water of life.

to water with one's tears *to wet by constant weeping*

- Mothers water the graves of their children with their tears.

water under the bridge *past history; no longer important*

- The joys and sorrows of my grandmother's life are now just water under the bridge.

to write on water or sand *to fail to leave behind an abiding record*

- The great *yogis* wrote their lives on water.

WEATHER. to weather your storms *to face the difficulties in your life*

- She has weathered her storms with grace and dignity.

WISHY-WASHY. wishy-washy *thin and weak; diluted; of poor quality*

- Your proposal is all wishy-washy.

Y

YARDSTICK. by the yardstick of *according to any standard of measurement*

- Your success in life is measured by the yardstick of your bank balance.

YARN. to spin a yarn *to make a tale; to tell a sailor's story often having incredible elements*

- The confidence trickster spun a yarn to ask for money.
- The storyteller had an enviable capacity to spin a yarn.

YEA. yea and nay *positive and negative; yes and no*

- There is a yea and nay to every problem in life.

YIELD. to yield ground *to accept defeat, to give way*

- The old manager has yielded ground to the new one.

YOKE. to yoke together *to be bound together; to work in a team*

- Ideally, husband and wife are yoked together for success or failure, victory or defeat, joy or sorrow.

YORE. of yore *long time; in times past*

- This is a tale of yore.
- She used to visit us of yore when my mother was alive.

YOUNG. to be with young *to be pregnant*

- He gave his seat in the bus to a woman with young.

Young Turk *one of a body of Turkish reformers who brought about the revolution of 1908*

- India has many Young Turks today who ache for changes in the political set-up.

Z

Z. from A to Z *from beginning to end*

- Please read the book from A to Z.
- You can learn the A to Z of astrology from his book on the subject.

ZEAL. (with) zest and zeal *with great fervour, strong feeling, such as love, anger, passionate ardour*

- The youth club members worked with zest and zeal for the welfare of the poor.
- The volunteers' zest and zeal is wonderful to see.

ZENITH. to reach the zenith *to achieve the highest glory; to reach the greatest height*

- Buddhism in India reached its zenith under Ashoka the Great.

ZERO. zero hour *the exact time fixed for launching an attack or beginning an operation*

- Both the armies were poised for action as zero hour approached on September 3, 1939.
- As zero hour starts in Parliament, pandemonium breaks loose.

ZOOM. to zoom in *to get a closer view of*

- The camera crew zoomed in on the aircraft's wreckage.

Notes